"WHICH BIRD do you think has the most beautiful song, Howie?" A darkening of the sky had encouraged a chorus of excited twittering in the forest around them.

"Well, I like the veery, myself. But folks say the sweetest song of all was the hermit thrush."

"The hermit thrush? Why do they call it a hermit thrush?"

"It's a shy little thing. You'll hardly ever see it," he said. "I've never even heard it myself. In fact no one alive has heard it. It stopped singing long ago."

"Why?"

"Well . . . the story goes that it had such a beautiful song that one of the first Rulers of Maynor had one captured. He put it in a cage. As if you could own a bird or its song." Howic looked over his shoulder and lowered his voice.

"Poor thing died in a day. Ever since then, no one has heard a hermit thrush sing. But my grandmother said it was the sweetest sound. 'Like a waterfall going backward,' she used to say."

There was something familiar about the story. Yes, she was sure of it. Their father had told it to her and Reba. In the orchard. She remembered how the story had upset her, and how Reba had comforted her, assuring her that the bird would not be silent forever.

"Will it ever sing again?"

The Hermit Thrush Sings

Susan Butler

Published by
Dell Laurel-Leaf
an imprint of
Random House Children's Books
a division of Random House, Inc.
1540 Broadway
New York, New York 10036

Visit us on the Web! www.randomhouse.com/teens

Educators and librarians, for a variety of teaching tools, visit us at
www.randomhouse.com/teachers

ISBN: 0-440-22896-4

RL: 7.2

Reprinted by arrangement with DK Publishing, Inc.

Printed in the United States of America

February 2001

10 9 8 7 6 5 4 3 2 1

OPM

For my mother, who taught me to love
a good story

~

My deepest thanks to Iso, for his patience and support; to my
mother, brother, sisters, and my children, Hannah and Joe, for
their encouragement and feedback; to my wonderful extended
family and family of friends, for their kind suggestions; to two
young readers, David Beams and my nephew Arlo Hart, for
their timely enthusiasm; to my editor, Melanie Kroupa, for
teaching me that less is more; and Gina Feuerlicht, for keeping
up Leora's courage, as well as my own.

Thanks also to Pine Manor College (a community of inspiring
young women) for granting me the time to work on this book.

The Gate

"TEEUU, TEEUU."

"I hear you," Leora whispered, peering out through the old iron gate that separated her from the forgotten alleyway to the Edgeland.

The stone houses, built side by side around the edges of Village Three, formed a solid wall over which the low April sun could barely peek. But from this alleyway she could glimpse the new green of the bushes and trees in the Edgeland fields beyond. Through the narrow passage the sun sent a hopeful sliver of light that bounced off her locket and danced on the dark walls beyond the gate.

The sun also warmed the fragile webbing between the fingers of her left hand, which, outspread like the wing of a bird in flight, rested lightly on the cold bars of the gate.

"Teeuu, teeuu."

"Teeuu, teeuu, to you," she called back.

She could not see the bird, but she knew it was a veery. It was a common bird here in the central part of Maynor. Like other birds, it rarely ventured into the bare cobblestone streets and dark alleyways of the town itself. But on this morning, its call invited her out to its own spring-touched world beyond the village walls.

Leora tried to imagine what the Edgeland might look like. She pictured apple trees, the bright green of their new leaves glowing in the early-spring sun. And birds, darting from bush to bush, tiny flashes of yellow and gray. She even imagined the long-silent hermit thrush, flicking its tail as it hopped from stone to stone.

It was, of course, forbidden to venture beyond the walls of the town. Only the croptenders, with their grim escort of guards, were allowed beyond the fortress-like wall that ringed the village. Leora shivered at the thought of always being watched by the guards. If only she could go out alone. . . .

Entranced by the veery's flutelike melody, she was unaware that her left hand had begun fingering the icy links of chain that held the gate closed.

"Leora!" Her stepsister's voice pierced the silence of the village behind her.

For a moment Leora's hand froze, exposed, the delicate webbing between her fingers translucent as a fish's fin, luminous against the morning sun. Then, as hastily as if her hand had been burned, she pulled it away and buried it in the dark folds of her cape.

"If you go out there the birmbas will eat you up and spit out your bones," Tanette taunted. "And besides," she added in her tattletale voice, "it is forbidden."

Leora cursed her carelessness in being caught looking out the gate, and, even worse, in exposing her left hand—especially today when her stepsister was accompanied by an after-school friend.

"But don't worry, Leora," Tanette added for the benefit of her friend. "Even the birmbas wouldn't eat your frog paw."

Flushing, Leora pulled her left hand farther into her cape. She held herself rigid as Tanette and her companion, their shoes echoing on the cobblestones, disappeared up the hill toward home.

Leora looked back out through the gate to the slit view of the distant Edgeland. Usually such an exchange with Tanette would have left her feeling numb and hopeless. Today, however, she was rescued by the appearance of the cinnamon-colored veery itself—jaunty, bright-eyed, pecking.

"Hello, veery," she said. "Guess what?"

The bird cocked its head inquiringly.

Leora lowered her voice. "The chain is broken."

The veery regarded her steadily with its beady eye.

"I could open the gate," she said in a hoarse whisper, as if the bird had been waiting for an explanation. "Anytime."

The veery gave her one last look, adjusted its wings, hopped twice, and flew off. As if to say, "What are you waiting for?"

Home

"TANETTE tells me you were trying to open an Edgeland gate."

"It has a chain, ma'am."

"Of course it has a chain. It's against the law to go into the Edgeland without the guards."

"Perhaps she wants to get eaten by the birmbas, Mummy," chimed in Tanette, her voice as sweet as you please.

Leora wanted to say that the birmbas were not in the Edgeland but in the forest beyond the Great Fence. But she never argued with Tanette.

"They gobbled up your father and your sister Reba," Tanette continued. "Maybe they like the taste of the Morans."

"You know it is forbidden, Leora, to go beyond the

village walls." Lady Blencher brushed an invisible speck of dust from her sleeve.

"And they will send you to the Institute if you disobey," Tanette went on. "Isn't that so, Mummy?"

The Institute. Leora's head flooded with a lifetime of rumors. Orphans, irregulars, delinquents. All kept in prisonlike conditions and forced to work at hard labor.

It was simply meanness for Tanette to mention it. Lady Blencher would surely never send her there. Nonetheless, the mention of it sent a chill down Leora's spine.

Lady Blencher did not respond. "Now, children," she said instead, "do you have any out-of-school work?"

"Yes, Mummy. We're to make a drawing."

"A drawing? Whatever for?"

"Teacher's niece, Miss Young, is visiting the class for a few days. Teacher let her give us our homework for the weekend."

"Well, that explains it. Run along, then. You'd best do what's asked of you. Your cousin Wilfert's arriving in town tomorrow with his troop. He'll have a chance to visit with us before he goes off on his first tour of duty. I want everything to be ready."

"Oh, Mummy," Tanette burst out. "Is Wilfert a real guard now?"

"Yes, dear. He graduated from the Guard Academy last month."

"Oh, wait till I tell them at school!"

Leora pulled her cape tightly about herself. It had been years since Wilfert, the nephew of her stepfather, the governor, had visited. She was haunted by the memory.

He had been playing with a slingshot when a bird had actually ventured into the village. Leora could remember the look in Wilfert's eye as he caught sight of it, perched innocently on their gatepost. She remembered the soft thud as his stone hit its mark, and how it had taken her breath away, as if she, too, had been struck. She could still see the tiny creature lying there, stunned, like a sleeping mouse.

Wilfert had put the bird into a box with bars on the front. Leora had gone later to look for it. She hadn't found it. But in a dark corner of the basement lay a scattered pile of feathers.

~

Leora was glad to escape to the warmth and clatter of the kitchen, still filled with the rich smells of Friday night's dinner. The plump figure at the stove turned to her.

"No mind," Norie said, as if reading in Leora's face her state of heart. "Take this." She pressed a warm berry tart into Leora's palm. "They're fresh done. And here's an extra one for later," she added, slipping another one into Leora's cape pocket.

Norie had been the family's nanny when Leora's father and sister, Reba, were alive. But after their death,

Leora's stepmother had remarried, and Norie had been demoted to cook. It was the kitchen that felt like Leora's home now.

"Howie, make some space there."

A short, solid man in work clothes and boots gave a mock salute and cleared some space on the counter. "Here you go," he said, kneeling with his hands clasped, inviting Leora to climb up, as she might using a stirrup, onto a horse.

Leora was glad to see Howie. He was Norie's beau, but usually he was away with the troops. Not as a guardsman but as a trail-chopper—clearing the way through the woods as the troops moved from one town to another.

"Some people," he said, nodding toward the living room, "should be fed to the gulls." Howie liked to talk about the sea. Before the Disaster, when the nation of Maynor was the state of Maine, his ancestors had lived off the sea. Leora knew he would have loved nothing better than to do the same. Though these days, neither he nor anyone else was allowed to go there.

"But gulls wouldn't have them, now I think of it," Howie went on. "I doubt they'd even do for lobster bait."

"Pshhhh!!" said Norie. "Keep your voice down, Howie. They don't like you settin' around here at the house. You know that." She slid another tray of un-baked tarts into the oven.

"Had to come here. On official business, you know. To bring the message about the troops and the arrival of . . ." Instead of saying Wilfert's name, Howie broke into a mock fit of coughing, snorting, and snuffling, as if the name of the person in question were too awful to mention. "Pay that swamp rat no mind," he whispered so that only Leora could hear him.

"Well, anyways," he continued out loud, "most important, I had to deliver a special item." He pulled a small, clumsily wrapped bundle from his pocket and handed it to Leora.

Leora, curious, unwrapped the rough package. A bird's nest!

"Blown down during the winter, I suppose. Almost stepped on it. Thought to myself, 'I know a little bird as would like that.' "

Leora wished she weren't so shy. She would have liked to thank Howie, but it was hard for her to muster even a thank you. She looked at him, hoping her eyes would say it for her. Then she cupped the nest in her hand, examining its delicate interweavings.

"I don't know what kind of bird it belonged to," he said, answering an unspoken question. "Your pa would've known. Knew everything there was to know, he did. Not just about birds. About every living thing."

Norie bumped hard against Howie and scowled as well as she could manage with her soft face. Leora knew Norie was trying to warn him away from the painful subject. But for some reason she never minded when Howie talked about her father.

"Who knows," continued Howie. "It might even have belonged to a hermit thrush. Ahhh, the hermit thrush," said Howie, winding up for a story. "Now there's an interesting bird! Hasn't sung for near a hundred years. Well, the story goes . . ."

Norie bumped against Howie again, this time with a look of alarm on her face. "Don't be talking forbidden talk, now!" she whispered. "And what's more, it's dinnertime."

"Another time," mouthed Howie to Leora with a conspiratorial wink. Leora put her bird's nest tenderly into one of her cape pockets, as Norie shepherded her as far as the dining room door.

On this night Lady Blencher's husband, the governor, was eating elsewhere. Throughout the meal, Tanette chattered happily with her mother. They did not talk to Leora, look at her, or expect her to speak. She might as well have been invisible.

But tonight she didn't mind. Under the dark folds of her cape, her webbed hand explored the twiggy texture of the bird's nest. Her mind was filled with thoughts of the jaunty cinnamon-colored veery. And with the memory of its invitation to the world beyond the gate.

Grand Nan

LYING IN BED, Leora could see the quarter moon out her window. She rubbed her locket. The cool feel of metal and chain reminded her of the lock on the Edgeland gate. She imagined she was looking at the moon from the other side of that gate.

She thought about Tanette and her friend, and how they had caught her with her webbed hand out of her cape. Most of the time Leora managed to feel nothing—neither sadness nor joy. But this feeling about her hand went back as far as she could remember. It was a feeling of dread. As if she did not belong here and was doomed to being discovered, singled out, and sent to some other dark world.

A creaking sound told her that Norie was on her way up the stairs. Although Leora's room was tiny and dim, and not so fine as the ones in the front of the house, she was glad it was next to Norie's and well removed from those of her stepfamily.

As the door opened, the room was lit by the dancing light of Norie's candle. "Not sleeping yet, are we?" she said softly from the doorway.

Leora knew Norie was anxiously studying her in the darkness.

"I've time for a tale if you like," Norie said.

Leora murmured assent. "A true tale tonight, Norie." And just to be sure that Norie steered clear of troublesome subjects, she added, "About Grand Nan."

Leora had only the dimmest memory of having heard the tale before. Although they'd learned about the Disaster in school, she knew that stories about the Before Time were forbidden to tell. And indeed Norie looked over her shoulder with an instinctive expression of alarm, before squeezing her comfortable form into the small rocker by the bed. Then she began a low "mmm-mmmmmm" sound, which went on for some minutes, with occasional stops and starts, as if she were telling the tale in her mind.

"It all began, of course, in the Before Time—which was, as you know, over a hundred years ago." Norie spoke in a voice that was little more than a whisper, as if someone might be listening at the door. "Maynor was not a country then. It was something called the state of

Maine in a very big country. The United something-or-other it was.

"And were there Rulers?"

"Well, yes, there were Rulers of that whole big country then, but"—and here Norie's voice dropped even lower—"it is said that the Rulers were chosen by the people!"

"By the *people?*"

"Shhhh, Leora. It's forbidden talk. But, yes, by the people."

Norie continued. "And in those days, there were roads between the cities. And traveling machines with wheels that went from village to village, faster than a galloping horse."

"For the guards?"

"Oh, no! In those days the people were allowed to go from village to village. They could go wherever they pleased. There weren't any guards then, if you can imagine that."

"Wasn't it dangerous?"

"Ahhh. Remember there were no birmbas then. But I'm getting ahead of myself.

"The tale begins with your mother's mother's mother's mother, your Grand Nan. She lived in the next village over. Village Fifteen. Except then it had a real name, instead of just a number. Well, she lived with your great-great-granddad on a farm of sorts—

sheep and goats and whatnot. Loved the land, they say. And she liked to draw, you know, just like you. Saw beauty everywhere. And it wasn't just outside things she'd draw—it was things from inside her mind."

"She liked to draw," Leora murmured softly. Under the covers she opened and closed the webbed fingers of her left hand. Her drawing hand.

"Yes," Norie continued. "And they say that one day she set about to do a picture from her mind, and out comes this picture like she'd never done before: the sky all dark and smoky, houses burned, the land all scorched. Very upset, she was! And the more she looked at it, the more upset she got. She knew there was trouble ahead. Not just for here, but for everywhere."

Leora could see the picture in her own mind's eye quite clearly.

"But she . . . her hand . . . was . . . normal?" Leora found herself trying to imagine what her Grand Nan must have looked like.

"Least as I know. Or I should say, better than normal, on account of she could draw, like you.

"Well, next thing you know she started telling folks in the village that a disaster was on its way. That the whole village better start saving food and water, and they better make the town safe from fire. Most of 'em didn't believe her, of course. Can't say as how I hardly blame them.

"August, it was. Blueberry time. And in those days at harvesttime, folks would come from far away to help with the picking. I don't mean from other parts of the country. I mean from a *different* country. Foreigners. Brown-skinned folks, with straight black hair, and speaking some other language, not English like you and me."

As Leora thought about the people that Norie described, her hand felt as if it were drawing. She could see lines appearing swiftly beneath her charcoal, depicting a little brown-skinned girl who sat on a table and looked at her with laughing eyes. Leora wondered who she was.

"Well, for whatever reason, these foreign folk, they believed your Grand Nan's story about the Disaster. And where usually they'd get trucked up here around blueberry time, and leave after the picking—*migratory*, I believe they called them, like the birds—well, dozens of them, they decided to stay with your Grand Nan. They built shelters and stayed with her and her husband on the land for the better part of a year. And all the time working: building a reservoir for water, canning food, and trimming a wide stretch of land all about the farm, against fire.

"Most people in town thought she was crazy, of course. Though there must have been a few believers as came and pitched in.

"End of the next summer came, and still no Disaster.

People poking fun about her, you can imagine. Then, suddenly, the people who studied those things, they say a great meteor is on its way to the earth! But too late by then—not so much as a week to prepare. And sure enough, boom! All over the earth comes such a shaking, like a thousand earthquakes. And over the sea, half a continent is sunk in the blink of an eye, and everywhere else fires spread uncontrolled, across the face of the world. And such a smoke as darkened the sun for a year and more.

"Them that didn't die of the fire died of starvation and cold."

"And Grand Nan?"

"Well, she was fine, along with her husband and her helpers from away, and as many in the village as she was able to save. And sure, in lots of places here and there was pockets of folks as managed to survive. It was years before the smoke died down and the sun began to shine same as before.

"But it never was the same. It was like hundreds of years just wiped away. There'd been buildings tall as twenty pine trees, people said, and bridges bigger than villages. Even machines that could fly in the sky, if you can believe that. All of it forgotten, burned, rusted, destroyed. Nothing left but what was made of stone."

"But couldn't they make it the same again?"

"Well, the thing was, you see, after your Grand Nan's time, some folks with some very set ideas got in charge here in Maynor. These Rulers, they said it wouldn't be for the good of the people to make things just the way they used to be."

"But why?"

"Oh, they gave one reason and another. And what were the people to say? By then there was the birmbas. There didn't used to be no birmbas, not in the Before Time. There was bears, of course. And in other parts of the world there was apes. But the birmbas, a new-species like they call them, they're a little bit like each."

Leora thought about the life-sized picture at school of a towering birmba, paws prepared to strike, its sharp incisors bared, its great face wrinkled into a frightening mask of savagery.

"So anyway, before long, the people were surrounded by wild beasts in the woods, and only the Rulers' guards to protect them. The people didn't have much they could say about things being one way or another."

Leora thought with surprise that Norie was saying something almost critical of the Rulers.

"And then there was the food problem. Just like the Disaster brought on new-species animals like the birmba, it brought on new-species plants. The nitta berries, the barka nuts. All of them poison, you know. And these plants, they started to take over and crowd out the old grains and things. And without the old-time farm machinery, farming was that much the harder. The people depended on the Rulers to bring in extra food in the winter. Brought it in from the neighboring countries, the Rulers did.

"So anyway, like I say, needing the Rulers like that, for food and protection . . . well." Norie paused. "What were the people to say?" Her voice had become distant. After a minute of silence, as if coming suddenly to her senses, she covered her mouth. "Don't be listening to me, now," she whispered. "These old stories of the Before Time, and of your Grand Nan, they're forbidden-to-tell. It's just between you and me, now. Let me tuck you in. They'll be missing me downstairs."

When Norie left, Leora had something new to think about.

She had never heard anyone say anything bad about the guards or the Rulers. Not that Norie had exactly said anything bad.

To think that at one time people could go freely wherever they pleased! No gates. No guards. No birmbas.

And no mutations, Leora thought as she pulled her left hand from under the covers. When her fingers were close together, it looked very much like her right hand. Usually she avoided looking at it. Tonight she held it up and spread her fingers against the moonlight. The filmy webbing dissolved the edges of the moon into a dull radiance.

Tomorrow she would draw a picture with this hand.

A picture her Grand Nan would have been proud of.

At the Window

LEORA REACHED the rear pantry by way of the back stairs. The tiny room was behind the kitchen across a narrow hallway. More than once, from here, she had heard conversations never intended for her ears.

She sat in her usual place on the wide shelf beneath the pantry window, her back propped against the wall, easily ignoring the clanking of dishes and rattling of pans as Norie and the new kitchen girl began preparing supper.

Few windows in the village looked outward as this one did. It was as if the village were simply turning its solid back on the outside world. Turning its back on nature itself. Saying to the fields and the forest, "Stay out." And saying to its people, "Stay in."

It was a good place for daydreaming. Sometimes she would select a particular tree in the distance and imagine that she were that tree. She imagined the sun on her leaves and the whispering of all the trees among themselves.

She wondered how she knew the sound of trees in the wind. Her little window did not open. And even if it did, she couldn't have heard a sound like that from here. A vast expanse of low brush surrounded the village. Only past that could one see the distant fruit trees of the Edgeland. And at a greater distance still was the dense dark green of the evergreens in the forest beyond.

Although she couldn't actually see it from here, Leora knew that the Edgeland was separated from the forest by miles and miles of iron fence. The Great Fence, she knew, had been built to keep out the birmbas. Only the guardsmen were allowed beyond it.

Now, as she looked from her perch, Leora spotted a band of croptenders and guardsmen returning to the village. The farmers, in homespun shirts, were carrying their tools. The guardsmen, in their bright uniforms, had guns at the ready.

Leora tried to make out who the croptenders were. She did not even bother trying to recognize any guardsmen. The guardsmen were always "from away," and were never stationed in one place for long enough to get familiar with the townspeople.

Only the week before she had seen them dragging a villager from his house—a trail-chopper, she later learned, who had been telling things that were forbidden-to-know.

Leora knew the guards were supposed to be there for the good of the people. Yet whenever she crossed paths with them she tucked her left hand even farther into her cape, as if the sight of her hand might make them arrest her and send her away.

With a shiver, Leora turned her eyes down to the piece of blank paper on her lap. She wanted to do her best work for Teacher's niece. Miss Young was friendly and cheerful and had already learned all the pupils' names.

Today, as Leora imagined the fields and trees of the Edgeland, a gnarled old birch began to appear beneath her pencil.

Norie was the only person ever to have seen Leora's drawings, having come across a secret collection of them under the bed one day in her cleaning.

"It's so real you can smell it," she had said at that time. "You have the gift of an angel. Have you shown your drawings to your teacher?"

Leora had thrust her hand deep into her cape, and Norie had said no more about it. But ever since, Leora had been able to count on the occasional appearance beside her bed of odds and ends of drawing paper, bits of charcoal, and, one time, even a quill and ink.

The paper Leora drew on now was heavy and soft,

with a fiber she could feel with her fingertips. Paper like this could not be bought in the village. Leora knew that Howie must have brought it "from away"—perhaps it was even from somewhere outside of Maynor.

What appeared as she drew was often a surprise to Leora herself. She smiled now as two squirrels, scurrying around the birch tree, appeared beneath her pencil. And a background of fir trees, and a tangle of willow and rhodora, and . . . what was this? It was a pair of eyes, almost invisible, peering out from within the brush! How strange!

Leora was so lost in her task that at first she was unaware that the din of pots had stopped, and that Norie and her new helper were talking in the kitchen across the passageway.

But then she heard Norie saying, "Her mother died of the plague not long after Leora was born. All broke up, her pa was. People said he only remarried to give his girls a ma. Everyone knew he was still mourning the girls' mother. And none like *her* for sure. The new stepmother, who already had one of her own, well, she treated the children all right to begin with.

"Then the tragedy! Leora's pa and sister got killed by the birmbas! Leora's real sister—Reba, her name was— I'm not sure she wasn't the lucky one, dying with her pa. Eaten, bones and all, they say. Leastwise they looked for weeks, and never found a thing. And him, his bones was all they found. Licked clean by those horrible beasts.

"Well, anyway, Lady Blencher, as her stepmother likes to be called, she set her eye on the governor straight away, and that was that. They were married within the year, and he moved here into the old house with her. Since then, the child's just a nuisance to her. And her own daughter, Tanette, well, that one was mean to Leora from the start."

"And the hand?"

"The hand? That hand of hers. It doesn't help. Lady Blencher thinks it an embarrassment. By the usual rule, the child would have been sent to the Institute at birth, but her pa would have none of it. I think her ladyship would be a mite ashamed to do it now."

"Poor little thing." The new housemaid's voice had moved from curiosity to genuine concern.

"It's a pity all right. Oh, Lord! Hear that?" Norie's voice lowered. "It's Leora. In the pantry. Heard every word. Me and my mouth. Here, dear, you finish these for me. I better go make it right."

But Leora was already in the front hallway, clutching her webbed hand to her body like a broken wing.

She let the door slam behind her and ran. The words followed her down the hill.

Out the Gate

WELL, IT DIDN'T REALLY MATTER. Nothing really mattered. And as far back as she could remember, nothing ever had.

She couldn't remember her father. She couldn't remember her sister. And she certainly couldn't remember her mother.

A few times at bedtime Norie had tried to start a conversation about all of that. But Leora didn't want to hear about it and would pretend to fall asleep.

Leora found herself, now, standing before the old rusty gate. She hadn't meant to come here. She certainly wasn't intending to go *out* of the gate. But just then she heard the sound of guards' boots on the cobblestones behind her. It was not just the familiar sound of a pair of guards walking. It was the heavy clomp clomp of a whole troop.

Wilfert! Surely this would be his regiment. She'd rather die than have him see her. But there was nowhere to hide. Her hand flew to the broken chain and unwound the heavy links. With all her weight she heaved open the gate, then swung it closed behind her.

She threw herself around the corner and up against the rear of the buildings. There she froze as the regiment marched rhythmically past.

Standing with her back to the cold brick wall, and her face in the sun, her fear gradually subsided.

"Teeuu, teeuu."

The veery! It strutted now from under a bush, pretending to peck for food, but in truth inspecting this new arrival.

"I told you the chain was broken," Leora whispered.

The veery eyed her, pecked the earth, skittered forward, then paused again, chest out and head cocked.

"I have a bird's nest," Leora said softly. "I'll show it to you sometime."

The bird came closer. Leora stood still as a mouse. She had never had any friends. Because of her hand, she supposed. But the veery didn't care about her hand. And somehow she was not surprised that it would trust her.

Now the bird pecked at a mound of pale moss, disentangled one of its blue-green threads, and shook it. With its prize in its beak, it eyed Leora for some seconds. And then in a flash, it spread its wings and flew off toward the Edgeland.

"Ohhh. Don't go," Leora said. It would be taking the bit of moss to make its nest. She longed to follow. Before her she could see what must have once been a path, beginning at the gate, and winding toward the higher shrubs and trees of the deeper Edgeland. A carpet of tiny bunchberry shoots and other young growth told her that the trail was not in use.

Forbidden, whispered the darkness of the village behind her. *Forbidden, forbidden, forbidden.*

The path in front of her, however, was lit by sunlight and flecked with bits of early-spring green. And the veery, she was sure, had invited her there.

So step by step, with her heart pounding, Leora moved forward.

The moss lit up the otherwise drab landscape. In some places, on close inspection, colonies of tiny single-leaf plants were beginning to peek above ground—some rolled, some open and delicately erect. She paused at a bend in the path. A cluster of low fir trees blocked her view of what lay beyond. She hesitated. Perhaps she should turn back.

"Teeuu, teeuu," the veery prompted from ahead.

Leora wanted to join the bird, but her feet felt

rooted. Had she been here before? She imagined that she knew what she would find beyond the bend: a clearing, and a great rock beneath an apple tree.

"Teeuu, teeuu."

What would the veery think if she turned back now? Perhaps it would never invite her again. Leora took the next few steps through the opening between the chubby firs.

She *had* been here before! There was the gnarled apple tree! There was the lichen-covered rock!

Memories long buried surged into her mind and body. As if it had been only yesterday, she recalled herself solidly stationed on her father's lap.

Entranced, she moved toward the great rock beneath the familiar tree. How they had managed to come here she did not know. But it had been here that they sat. And here that he had told her stories. About each flower, each bird, and each tree.

The surge of memory was clear and detailed. The last time they had sat here, her father had been so engrossed in talking about the birds that the setting of the sun must have gone unnoticed.

It had been a sound in the woods that seemed to have brought him to his senses. He had picked her up and run, as if for their very lives, back down the path, through the undergrowth and into the village.

Leora sat down now in that old sitting place on the

rock. "Papa," she said softly. "Oh, Papa!" And then it was as if all the tears she'd ever refused to cry swelled up and overflowed.

When at last Leora stopped crying, a chorus of twittering in a nearby bush told her the veery was not alone. She hadn't noticed the earthy smell of the air. She took in deep, slow breaths, feeling its freshness.

Pushing aside the crushed mat of dry leaves at her feet, she discovered a host of tiny mayflower shoots, just readying themselves to peek out into the sunlight.

And there was the veery, perched on the apple tree.

"Is this your orchard?" she asked. "Are you waiting for spring?"

"Teeuu, teeuu."

How would all this look in another month? Perhaps she would not spend all her time within the village walls this spring.

Leora's imaginings were interrupted by a sound. The sound of something approaching through the shrubby woods. Something large, moving quickly.

Was this the same alarm her father had felt when he rushed her back to the village so long ago?

Although she could not see it, she knew very well what it must be: a birmba!

Leora knew she should run for her life. But she might as well have been glued to the rock.

Spreading her webbed fingers, she shaded her eyes against the low-hanging sun and looked toward the sound of the crackling branches. As if on signal, the sound stopped. Even the birds grew silent.

Slowly it came to her that she was looking into a pair of eyes—animal eyes—barely discernible in the tangle of bushes and fir trees. Like the eyes she had drawn in her picture!

"Birmba," she whispered.

The strangest thing of all was that her petrifying alarm was being gently replaced by an odd sense of peace. She felt comforted, and quite safe.

"Birmba," she whispered again.

And then, into the silence, she whispered, "I'm Leora."

Her eyes met the eyes in the woods. As their gazes locked, she felt something flowing between them. But she could put no words to it. The birds were quiet, the wind was still, not a twig snapped. At last she blinked, and, as suddenly as they had appeared, the eyes in the woods vanished.

Had she imagined it? Was it a birmba? Why hadn't it hurt her? What did it want?

"It *was* a birmba," she said to the veery, which was eyeing her now from an elderberry bush. "I know it was."

But there was no time to stand and wonder about it.

The sun was sinking. It was time to return to the village.

And to Wilfert.

Her eyes sought out the veery on its perch, memorized the contours of the trees and the smooth lines of the lichen-covered rock.

"I will come again," she said out loud.

Wilfert

LEORA'S FIRST STEPS into the house cast a cold shadow over the afternoon's pleasure. She hesitated. Then, standing on the unwelcoming threshold, an odd thing happened. The familiar hallway and furniture took on an unexpected new life. The walls and doorways and tables and chairs seemed again to be the ones that had been part of her home here with her father and her sister, Reba. It was over there that her father had hung his overcoat. And there on that bench where she had sat while Reba, seven years her senior, had helped her tug off her winter boots. And there in that empty space above the table had hung a portrait of their mother.

As her eyes explored the hallway, something on the entry table brought her rudely back into the present. It was a hat. Just a hat. But the sight of it made her skin prickle. The hat belonged to Wilfert. She was sure of it. And it lay on the table just where Reba's gloves once would have lain.

She became aware of muffled voices from the darkened end of the long central hallway. Were they coming from the basement? The door to the dank basement of the house was rarely opened. But it was certainly open now, and Leora could make out voices.

". . . first time in captivity . . ." she made out. Then, ". . . secrecy . . . utmost importance . . ."

One of the voices she recognized as Wilfert's. A louder, more authoritative voice was unfamiliar. "Don't be deceived—it's small, but it could kill a grown man. We have to get it to the government laboratory. Alive."

A third voice said something about ". . . tomorrow afternoon . . ."

Before Leora could get out of sight, two heavy-booted guardsmen emerged from the basement door and headed for the front hall. When they spotted her, they stopped without a word and scowled. She moved out of the doorway as the two strode past her, shutting the front door firmly behind them.

Leora hurried down the hall toward the kitchen, hoping to escape a confrontation with Wilfert. But there he was, his red-coated back toward her, as he closed and locked the basement door. The key in the lock made an unpleasant grinding and clunking sound.

"You!" he said as he turned around. Then he rushed away, tucking the key into his pocket as he went.

She put her ear against the basement door. What was down there?

~

In the lulls in the dinner conversation, the clinking of cutlery and china was particularly loud. Leora had chosen a chair as far away as possible from Wilfert. Even so, she could hear him breathing.

Tanette's gaze rarely left her cousin's face. She clearly would have liked to talk to him, but her mother's admonishing look demanded silence.

Leora looked steadily at her own plate, but from time to time she could feel the chill of Wilfert's eyes upon her.

The last time he had visited, some years ago, she had become so attuned to the timing of his cruelty that she could anticipate exactly when to expect it. She felt that way now as she sensed him trying to catch her eyes and hold them.

"I'll have those potatoes," he said evenly. He never referred to her by name, but she knew he was speaking directly to her. It had always been one of his games to try to make her expose her webbed hand. He knew full well that it would take both her hands to pass the heavy tureen.

Tanette, eager to please, and missing the point of Wilfert's game, reached to pass the tureen herself.

"No, Tan. Don't you bother," he said sharply.

Without looking up, Leora knew he was staring at her. She knew that with his eyes he was saying, "I can make you do it."

She felt herself shrinking within. In the inner pocket of her cape, her webbed fingers began curling up upon themselves. But as they did so, they brushed against the dried grassy texture of her bird's nest, its matted twigs, its soft mossy crevices.

Suddenly, it was as if it was not herself but the bird's nest she was protecting. The bird's nest and everything in the world it belonged to. And for the first time in her life she looked steadily back at Wilfert. The message she gave him with that look, which he could not fail to understand, was, "I will not. You cannot make me."

The kitchen door opened behind her.

"The potatoes." Wilfert's voice was louder now.

Leora felt her face flush, but she didn't look away.

"The potatoes, sir?" Norie asked, setting down a basket of fresh bread. She lifted the tureen and bustled around to Wilfert's side. "Shall I serve you, sir?"

"Maybe later," Wilfert replied, casting a dark look in Leora's direction.

Leora retreated within herself and was soon lost in memories of dinners past. Dinners with her father and Reba. Dinners accompanied by interesting talk, and laughter and giggles. Had she really ever been that person? A person with a family of her own?

By the time her mind drifted back to the table, the governor was talking with Wilfert about government affairs.

Although Leora usually ignored such adult talk, Norie's tale about the Before Time had made her curious.

"A silly effort, of course," the governor was saying to Wilfert. "The rebels are helpless. For one thing, the birmbas make it impossible to travel and communicate between villages. So the rebels can't organize. For another, our strategy of consolidating the winter food supply means the people would starve without the government to feed them. Thirdly, of course, they have no weapons.

"And then," he added, "there's the fourth defense." The governor paused. "Mutual suspicion," he whispered so low that Leora could barely hear.

"It's common knowledge," the governor concluded. "They don't stand a chance."

What, Leora wondered, did it mean to be a *rebel*?

Wilfert, clearly, was not persuaded by his uncle's assurances. "But Village Fifteen, sir—they say it's getting out of hand, sir. Some say it should be put down before it goes too far. Sir."

Wilfert continued in heated little bursts. "Where treason is concerned . . . well, there's no saying where it will stop . . . and the Rulers must be protected. Well . . . death would be too kind. Sir."

"Village Fifteen, you say," the governor mused.

"Oh, Wilfert," Tanette interjected. "Have you been to all the villages? I shall tell them at school."

"Not all. Only the ones of *significance*, Tan," Wilfert said, squaring the shoulders of his red coat.

"Well, what is Village Fifteen like? Oh, do tell me. Is it fancy? Is it better than here at Village Three?"

They all knew, of course, that things about other villages were forbidden-to-tell, that he would only relate what was common knowledge.

"Well, Tan," Wilfert said, relaxing into a tone of full authority, "the people are brown skinned and dark eyed." He paused as if this in and of itself were a crime.

"Secretive and disobedient," he went on, saying the words as if by rote.

"And in private," Wilfert continued, "they speak a language—well, not English. Which is forbidden, of course. They're not the sort of citizens the Rulers can count on.

"In fact if it weren't for . . . one particular person . . . the lot of them would have perished in the Disaster."

Leora remembered Norie's story, about the brown-skinned people "from away." The people who had believed in her Grand Nan's vision, and helped prepare with her for the Disaster.

Tanette's eyes had opened wide. This was clearly something she did not know about. Perhaps something forbidden-to-know. And indeed Wilfert did not elaborate.

"It's not for me to say, of course," said Wilfert, glancing at his brass buttons, "but if Village Fifteen burned right to the ground . . . some people would say it was for the good of the nation."

Leora shivered. Her hand fluttered, and wrapped itself protectively around the small rough nest in her pocket. She was relieved when Lady Blencher excused her and Tanette from the table.

～

As Leora lay under her covers that night, her mind was crowded with pictures: of the apple tree, in full leaf, as she had seen it long ago; of her father's eyes, alive with pleasure as he told her stories about animals, birds, and things that grew in the woods.

One of the clearest pictures was of her sister, Reba. Her big sister. Her *real* sister. She could see her, with her wild red hair blowing in the wind, climbing fearlessly to the uppermost branches of the tallest tree. Reba, she remembered their father saying, could climb like a mountain cat and outrun the deer.

Fingering her locket, Leora remembered something else. Reba had worn a special locket, like her own. She could see Reba holding it high above her head toward the sky, where it would catch the light of the sun and shine radiant as a star.

Visit to the Basement

THE SOUND HUNG in the air. A distant muted cry. Or had she dreamed it? All was quiet, except for Norie's rhythmic snore on the other side of the wall.

There it was again! The cry of something in distress. Before she knew it she was out from under her quilt, her feet on the floor, her wool cape about her. In the dark her hand found the doorknob.

The sound of Norie's bed creaking stopped her momentarily, but as soon as the steady snore resumed, she moved step by step down the hallway. The window at the end of the hall cast a pale light on the steps down to the kitchen. Leora could smell last night's dinner as she felt her way carefully down the winding stairs. At the landing below she paused and listened. Silence.

No. There! She heard it again, ever so softly this time, a plaintive moan. Hastily she found and lit a candle in the kitchen. She found the spare key that had hung for years on a peg in the pantry. Gripping it tightly, she hesitated for a moment in front of the basement door.

Leora had shunned the basement ever since years before when Wilfert had imprisoned the bird there. Now, as she opened the door, she felt the cool dank air from below and inhaled a still-familiar musty smell. As she started down the stairs there was no sound but the muffled pat of her slippers, step by step.

Then something scrabbled below. With her heart pounding, she looked in the direction of the sound. There, crouched behind the bars of a crudely caged-in corner was . . . could it be? It must be! A *baby birmba*! So frightened it looked as if it were trying to enter the wall itself. And yet the position of its legs left it perfectly prepared to spring forward in ferocious attack.

The beast's tiny round eyes glowed in the candle-light. Its little teeth showed beneath a pulled-up lip, its hair stood on end, and the moaning sound became a fearsome hissing and snarling.

Perhaps she had made a mistake coming down here alone. But something made her stay. She crouched a few feet away from the cage and stared at the little birmba, which stared right back at her.

Gradually she became aware of the sound of dripping water. Remembering the old stone sink in the basement, she rose, washed a grimy discarded cup, and filled it to the brim with water.

"Here, little birmba." Leora crouched back down and put the cup between the bars.

Teeth bared and snarling, the birmba maintained its threatening posture.

"Where's your mama?" At the thought of the animal being taken from its mother, Leora reached her right hand through the cage in sympathy. The birmba neither advanced nor recoiled. Leora felt hypnotized by the glowing eyes. It seemed they would stay like that forever.

Finally her hand grew tired. On an impulse, she loosened her cape and put her webbed hand tentatively through the bars, while she made a low, wordless cooing sound.

As if by magic, the birmba's glossy fur settled down. It lowered its lip over its teeth, and softened its stance. Its eyes got wider than Leora thought possible. It was so transformed that it didn't occur to Leora to withdraw her hand as the animal scuttled over to the cup and lapped it dry.

This done, it eyed Leora intently. Leora resumed her deep-chested coo. She wished she had something to feed it. Then she remembered. She had never eaten the fruit tart that Norie had put in her cape pocket. She put the crumbling, sticky handful between the bars. The animal snatched the tart quickly. With deft little four-fingered hands, it popped the pastry bit by bit into its mouth, cheeks bulging and jaw rolling, staring steadily at Leora all the while.

Leora rubbed her left thumb over the tips of her webbed fingers, making a soft brushing sound, and reached a little closer. The baby birmba, finished with its meal, turned as if to walk away, but then, to her surprise, scooted itself abruptly backward so that Leora's hand found itself positioned on the back of the animal's neck.

Suddenly Leora felt its silky fur beneath her webbed fingers—fingers that had hardly ever touched a living creature. But she seemed to know quite well what was needed by the birmba, as she stroked, scratched, and kneaded the velvety neck and ears.

"What shall I call you, little birmba?" she asked as the little creature nestled into a comfortable ball beneath her hand.

"Wiggala," she answered herself. "I'll call you Wiggala."

The creature wasted no time snuggling up as close as possible to her, settling himself on his haunches, curling his little hand tightly around one of her fingers, and falling fast asleep.

School

"IF YOUR PICTURE'S anything like your handwriting, Leora . . ." Tanette gave a snorting little laugh and looked around for signs of amusement from the other children, all with their homework in hand, who crowded toward the schoolhouse doorway.

Leora flushed. It was true that her writing, penned with her normal, right hand, was practically illegible. Privately, she had tried using her left hand, and had easily produced an elegant flowing script. But that was of little use to her in the schoolroom.

In any event, between criticism for her poor penmanship and rebuke for her tendency to daydream, Leora had nothing but dread for school.

As the children arrived on this morning, there was a general air of pleasant anticipation about Teacher's niece. Teacher, who would be conducting the class until recess, was stationed sternly at her desk at the front of the room. But Miss Young was at the doorway, greeting each child cheerily by name as she received his or her work.

"Good morning, Tanette. Thank you very much." Leora, following Tanette, saw her stepsister pause and search Miss Young's face for some token of special attention—special attention routinely given her by Teacher herself. But Tanette searched in vain. Teacher's niece was clearly unaware that Tanette was the governor's daughter!

"And good morning to you, Leora. Thank you very much," Miss Young said as Leora handed her the assigned picture. It must have been the special weight and feel of the paper that made Miss Young pause and glance down.

Surprised, she studied the graceful lines of the gnarled birch, the lifelike renditions of the scampering squirrels. Although it was hardly likely she noticed the pair of eyes buried in the leafy texture of the background, perhaps she noticed the veery hidden in a bush.

"Why, Leora. This is the loveliest picture. Look, children," she exclaimed, holding the ivory page up for all to see. "After your recess, we'll spend some time talking about drawing. I think we can all learn something from Leora."

Teacher contracted her brow, clearly not pleased by this praise. Leora averted her eyes and hurried to her seat. She was happy that Miss Young liked her drawing, but tried to ignore the looks of surprise on the faces of her classmates. She pretended to busy herself with her books, and soon her mind was far away.

It had been difficult to leave the house this morning. She sat now, thinking about the baby birmba—his large round eyes, his soft fur, the feeling of his tiny paw curled about her finger.

The guards had said something about a government laboratory.

How would they get the baby there? And what would they do to it? Only one sad fact was certain: Whatever they intended, there was nothing she could do to stop them.

~

When Leora's attention drifted back to the classroom, the science lesson was in progress.

"And what's another characteristic of amphibians, children?" Teacher intoned.

"Webbed feet," said a boy in front.

"Webbed hands," chimed in Tanette in her sweet-as-pie voice.

Leora flushed. Clearly she had provoked the extra wrath of her stepsister this morning by winning Miss Young's praise. She froze, trying to will herself, for the millionth time in her life, into invisibility.

As she retreated inward, it occurred to her that Wiggala hadn't minded her hand.

But what good was she or her hand to Wiggala if she couldn't even prevent the guards from taking him away? Tomorrow afternoon, the guards had said. By the time she got home from school, the little creature would be gone!

Now the class was working its way through the mammals, and Teacher was unrolling a picture on the wall.

"And what is this, children?"

There was the familiar image of an immense shaggy creature, something between bear and ape, its cruel teeth bared, its great clawed paws ready to attack. Leora had difficulty reconciling the tiny, mean eyes with the wide ones she had imagined she saw in the brush.

"Birmba," all voices sang out in unison, with a tinge of excitement.

"And what do we know about birmbas, children?" The tone in her voice hinted that if they were disobedient, the fierce creature in the picture might step right off the wall and teach them the answer.

"They kill people," several voices said.

"They *eat* people!" sang Tanette.

"They're carnivores," chanted a boy in the back. "And they are a new-species," he added, clearly unwilling to stop at one correct answer.

"And what is a new-species?" Teacher said, selecting one of the raised hands.

"It's a mutation," the girl answered, flashing a look toward Leora.

Leora fell still. She felt trapped and helpless, exposed like one of the butterflies pinned to the board on the schoolroom wall.

"A mutation that turned into a whole new species," the girl continued, "caused by a meteor hitting the earth in the Disaster."

"And how did a meteor produce the new-species?" Again, the thinly veiled suggestion that if they didn't know the answer, the Disaster would strike again on the spot.

This time the room was silent.

"Have we learned this before, children?"

"Yes, Teacher," the class droned obediently.

"Miss Young," said Teacher, "let's tell the children. Shall we?"

Teacher's invitation left it unclear whether Miss Young was a fellow teacher or simply a somewhat older pupil.

"Why, certainly. It's such a complicated thing," Miss Young said. "The Disaster destroyed big power-making facilities, causing the accidental release of a great deal of something called *nuclear energy*. Nuclear energy causes the release of something called *radioactivity*. And radioactivity can cause changes in species called *mutations*—major mutations such as the new-species, or very minor changes, such as a change in the color of a bird."

"People with mutations get sent to the Institute," volunteered Tanette.

Leora kept her eyes down, but she could feel all the students staring at her.

"Unfortu—" Miss Young caught herself midword and began again. "That's generally the case," she said shortly, moving back against the wall, as if she were relieved to turn the class back over to Teacher.

Teacher, with a cold look at her niece, launched purposefully into a civics lesson.

Leora did her best to put herself back into her familiar state of stony oblivion. But she found herself captive to the collective drone of the class.

"Obedience to the Rulers . . ." the children chanted dutifully in answer to the first question.

". . . because it's the law . . . because it's forbidden . . ." they intoned to the next ones.

". . . obedience-to-the-Rulers-because-it's-the-law-because-it's-forbidden . . ." the dirge wore on.

Leora wondered why they never mentioned the greatest "forbidden" of all: forbidden-to-know.

Were these lessons the same for the children in Village Fifteen? But she knew the answer to that. It was "sure as the dough rises," as Norie would have put it: For all the children in all the schoolrooms in all the villages, the questions and the answers were always the same. And always would be. It was the law.

～

When recess came, Leora could not wait to escape.

Over the din of children playing, she could hear

Tanette boasting loudly about "Cousin Wilfert the Guard."

What, Leora wondered, was Wilfert doing now? Were the guards in the basement at this very minute?

Would they put Wiggala in a tiny cage—trapped, terrified, and exposed?

Would they bind and truss his little arms, leaving him vulnerable and helpless?

Well, they just couldn't! Maybe Wiggala was helpless. But she certainly was not!

She did not care that it was the middle of the school day. She did not care about Teacher, or Tanette.

She did not know what she would do. But she would do something.

Walking swiftly out the school-yard gate and up the hill toward the house, she felt uncommonly strong.

Release

LEORA OPENED THE FRONT DOOR and paused to listen for household sounds. All was silent.

The basement key was on the peg where she had left it. She hoped that no one was in the house to hear the metallic turning of the key in the lock.

Closing the door softly behind her, Leora felt her way down the stairs. There was not a sound to be heard. A single tiny window cast a meager light into the caged area of the basement. Nothing moved. Had they already taken the baby birmba away?

"Wiggala?" she whispered. Her eyes made out a mound in the corner of the cage. It did not move. Her fear that the baby birmba had been taken away was replaced by a deeper dismay that he might be dead.

"Wiggala," Leora said, reaching through the bars for the furry form. Her right hand told her that the creature was warm and must be alive. But it was her webbed left hand, stroking the soft fur, that seemed to be bringing life back into the crumpled body.

There was a thud above. The front door! It was followed by the heavy tromp of footsteps. Was a guard coming to get Wiggala? Leora looked desperately about the basement for a place to hide.

The old cupboard. Of course. She had hidden there in games of hide-and-seek with Reba, long ago.

As the key ground in the lock at the top of the stairs, she dove into her old hiding place, pulling the door behind her. It would not close tightly, but in the dim light of the basement perhaps no one would see. She herself could just make out the baby birmba, which was now moving slightly, and peering about as if dazed.

As the footsteps reached the last stair, the birmba snapped to life. He gave a low growl, bared his teeth, and backed into the farthest corner of the cage.

The red-coated figure of a guard came into view. The silhouette was all too familiar. So was the prickling feeling of her skin. Wilfert!

Was he going to tie the birmba up and take him away? It seemed unlikely. So what was Wilfert doing here?

He disappeared from her field of vision, reappearing with a discarded length of curtain rod. Now what? He inserted the end of the rod through the bars of the cage. As the tip of the rod advanced on Wiggala, the baby birmba reacted wildly, hissing, snapping, and cringing against the wall.

The sound that escaped from Wilfert was so nasty, it was hard to recognize as laughter. He retracted the rod and then pushed it through again as the baby animal cowered and bared his teeth.

For some seconds Leora's vision went black, as she struggled against the sick feeling in her stomach. She was on the verge of hurling herself at him when she was saved by the heavy clunk of the front door and the thumping of two new sets of boots in the hallway.

"Blencher!" came a muffled bark from above.

Wilfert retracted the rod and tore up the basement steps, slamming the door behind him. In the welcome silence Leora rushed to the cage. With weak fingers, she worked at the knotted rope that held the door closed, all the while making little noises of comfort.

"Wiggala, Wiggala," she cooed. At last the knot gave. The baby birmba was in her arms in a bound, his trembling arms about her neck.

"Wiggala," Leora whispered again, nuzzling his sleek head with her cheek. Clinging to her with all his might, he buried his face in her hair.

"What will we do? What will we do?" Leora crooned, using her own question as a lullaby of comfort. The light reflected off the creature's great round eyes, which were looking into her own with infinite trust.

Looking into those eyes, a picture surfaced in her

mind—a pair of eyes, peering out through the shrubbery of the Edgeland. Eyes that, like Wiggala's, had looked deeply into her own.

But of course! It must have been Wiggala's mother, out there in the orchard. Searching for her baby!

Now Leora knew exactly what she must do.

"Shhhh, shhhh," she said. "Don't worry." And she cuddled the silent creature clasped in her left arm, comforting him as if he were a crying child.

"We have to hurry," she said, wrapping her broad woolly cape tightly around the baby birmba. "We have to find your mama."

~

Later, Leora had no memory of having left the basement, or of walking through the vacant town streets. She could not even remember slipping through the old iron gate.

It wasn't till she had rounded the bend of the Edgeland path that she came to herself.

Although it had been only the day before that she had rediscovered this Edgeland world, it seemed familiar and welcoming. Her eyes drank in the winter grays and olive greens, the vivid spring green of the moss.

She took a deep breath, pulling the sweet air into her lungs. She could feel the expansion and contraction of the birmba's tiny chest. As she loosened her cape to uncover his glossy head, he lifted his face from her shoulder and swiveled his head, surveying the world with widened eyes.

An orchestra of twittering greeted them. A flock of small birds flitted from bush to bush, inspecting the new arrivals from a variety of vantage points.

"Teeuu, teeuu," the veery called from somewhere nearby.

"We did it, Wiggala," Leora cried triumphantly, as she spied the apple tree. "We're home."

The orchard, really, was home to neither of them. But Leora could think of no better plan than to wait there and hope that the mother birmba would eventually appear to claim her lost baby.

Rationally, Leora knew that this was hardly likely. How, after all, could the baby's mother know they were there? And even if she found them, there was nothing to guarantee that she would not attack Leora, leaving only *her* bones to tell the tale.

But any fears about her own safety were overshadowed by the urgency she felt about delivering Wiggala to his mother.

So with the baby in her arms, she settled herself beneath the apple tree and waited.

The smaller birds skittered ever closer and soon were pecking for bugs among the matted leaves close about them.

Leora kept up a low, modulated sound, not really music but an instinctive ongoing hum of reassurance, a sort of wordless lullaby. Wiggala, watching the brush, turned from time to time to study his protector.

After a time, Leora noticed a change in her young charge. His small body tensed, his little ears standing up straight as he looked off into the greenery. Then he let out a long, low call, paused for a response, and called again.

Leora heard nothing, but the baby birmba's hold around her neck loosened. Gradually, without hearing or seeing her, Leora understood that the mother birmba was near. She could feel it. And strangely, she was unafraid.

Straining her eyes in the direction of Wiggala's gaze, she saw a movement in the shrubs. And there it was. None of her lessons at school or pictures in books had even begun to prepare her for the sight.

Leora stared in awe at the magnificent beast, its silky fur blowing in the gentle breeze. She marveled at the sense of power in its great form, and at the grace of its stance.

Now Leora was able to discern the mother's low call to its offspring, a sound so deep that Leora might not have perceived it as a sound at all.

It was with an odd mixture of happiness and sadness that she felt the little birmba gathering himself to leave her. His soft eyes met hers in farewell. He searched under her cape. His tiny paw found and stroked her webbed hand. Then, with a final squeeze of her finger, Wiggala was out of her arms.

Leora watched as he loped off into the low underbrush; watched as he reappeared moments later and hurtled himself into the furry enclosure of his mother's arms.

With Wiggala wrapped securely in her arms, Mama Birmba returned to her full stature. Leora stood up to meet the majestic creature's gaze.

She knew that with that silent look she was being thanked. She also understood that in the moment the previous day when their eyes had first connected in the orchard, this is what she had been asked to do.

Leora held up her webbed hand in acknowledgment and farewell as the mother and baby turned and disappeared.

~

Trudging back to the village gate, she sighed, burying her left hand back into its accustomed place.

She could hardly bear the thought that she might never see Wiggala again. But the pain shared space in her chest with an unfamiliar sense of fullness. In fact Leora felt so included in the warmth of the birmba reunion that she was unprepared for what awaited her in the place she herself had always called home.

Trouble

THE HOUSE was in an uproar. The front door was open, and from the path she could hear the sound of voices raised in disagreement. In the darkness of the front hall Leora could make out the figures of two guardsmen, Lady Blencher, Wilfert, and Tanette.

"With all due respect," the lieutenant was saying, "I think it's unlikely that the child is guilty. It took four grown men to capture that wild thing in the first place —armed with staffs and a noose and a good deal of courage."

"But," objected Wilfert, "Tan says Leora left school early. And Tan says she's seen her trying to open the gate."

Leora froze at the doorway.

It was Tanette who spotted her.

"There she is," she singsonged triumphantly. "There she is!"

Silence fell as all eyes turned upon her.

"Leora," said Lady Blencher, her voice ominously level.

Leora could do nothing but step inside.

"Something unfortunate has happened, Leora," said Lady Blencher steadily, her lips tight. "Our troops managed to capture a young birmba. It was being held in our basement until it could be taken to the capital for our scientists to study. I am hoping you had nothing to do with its disappearance."

Leora, silent, could hear the lieutenant whispering to the captain, ". . . shrimpy little thing like her . . . couldn't have done it . . . waste of time . . ."

"I have to ask you now, Leora," Lady Blencher was saying. "Did you release this animal?"

Leora had no intention of lying, but the word *yes* would not come out of her mouth.

Her silence, however, spoke for itself.

"She did it! She did it! She did it!" Wilfert's voice grew higher and shriller with each incantation.

"Well, I'll be . . ." muttered the lieutenant. "How in . . ."

"She did it, didn't she?" Tanette jostled her mother, as amazed as she was excited. "She did it!"

Lady Blencher's face colored. "You have been disgrace enough to this household, Leora," she said, her voice still controlled. "You will kindly tell the guards where you took it."

Leora kept a stony silence, her eyes on the ground. She was vaguely aware that Wilfert stood unpleasantly close. But her mind was on Wiggala and Mama Birmba, praying that each minute allowed them to get farther from danger.

"It's no use," the captain said at last. "We'll not be able to catch it anyway. It was a rare chance that let us capture it before. We're wasting our time. Let them deal with her at the Institute."

The Institute! Leora lifted her eyes in shock to her stepmother's face. Lady Blencher looked away. In that chilling moment, Leora understood that the issue had been discussed and decided even before her return, and that her stepmother had wished her at the Institute from the start.

Tanette herself was silent, wide-eyed, and stricken— as if this were a fate far worse than even she would have wished upon her stepsister.

"The basement would be the place to keep her till we leave." Wilfert's voice was cool as steel.

"Norie will take her to her room, Wilfert," said Lady Blencher uncomfortably.

"We'll be leaving for the capital tomorrow," the tall officer said. "We'll deliver her there."

"Tanette. Fetch the cook. Please hurry!" Lady

Blencher paced anxiously, as if she were terribly busy and had pressing business in some other room.

As Norie emerged from the kitchen, Lady Blencher, avoiding her eyes, spoke briskly. "Leora will be leaving for the Institute tomorrow. Please take her to her room."

Norie paled. For a few long seconds she stared speechlessly at Lady Blencher. Then she exploded. "The Institute! For shame! She was your own husband's flesh and blood! It'll be the death of her."

Lady Blencher, like a dry match catching fire, delivered a powerful slap to Norie's face. "The child's defective," she hissed.

Then she looked at the guards and flushed.

Norie's jaw was clenched, her eyes narrowed, as she inched closer to Leora.

"I still think that the basement would be the place to put her." Wilfert moved closer. "I'll get some answers out of her. We'll see what she has to say."

Hearing this, Norie swooped down on Leora, and, as if she were no more than an infant, heaved her up in her arms. "I'll take her to her room, madam." And with this she rushed her large bundle out of the guards' reach, up the stairs, and, panting, delivered her safely to the door of her room.

"The idea!" Norie puffed. "That phony highfalutin cockatoo! But you stay here now. I don't want that Wilfert laying a hand on you. I'll be back when I can."

The Institute. For the ones who were . . . different. Ir-regular. Disobedient. Bad. The ones who didn't belong.

That evening, whenever Norie's busy dinner sched-ule allowed, she appeared at the door, her eyes wild with worry, tears threatening to brim over. Leora was afraid Norie would hug her. She didn't want Norie to cry or carry on. She held herself rigid and avoided her eyes. There would be no feelings about this. None at all.

The food Norie brought her, Leora left untouched.

When Norie appeared after dinner, she had clearly taken Leora's cue about keeping feelings in check. She did her best to bustle about the room as if there were a great deal of important tidying to be done, though it seemed only a matter of time before the tears balanced on her lower lid would get the better of her.

"Harrumph." Howie hesitated at the doorway.

He looked quickly but searchingly at Leora, his brow knotted. Leora hoped that he too would spare her any uncomfortable talk.

"So I bumped into this fellow I know," he said, trying to sound casual, as if they had all been sitting around the kitchen chatting.

"A chopper, like me."

Howie's stocky form looked out of place in the tiny room.

"A good fellow. Just passing through town with his

troop, and in a rush." Howie eyed the little rocker, but thought better of it. "Last thing he tells me is that when he was to Village Fifteen, a young lady approaches him in the marketplace and asks him: Does he know the house at Village Three, the one on the hill? So he knows right away she means this one. So he says yeah, on account of he knows me to speak to. Well, turns out this young lady, she's inquiring 'bout the little one, *the one with the hand*, as he called her."

"Howie!" Norie rebuked him.

"Now, Nor. There's nothing wrong with her hand but what fools think. And it's fools have to live with their own foolishness."

Howie paused. Then continued. "Well, anyway, he tells me, this young lady, she's got this chain round her neck with a funny locket thing."

"The locket!" Norie gasped.

Leora sat bolt upright.

"Reba had a locket!" she exclaimed. "It was just like mine!"

She pictured the locket about Reba's neck. She could see Reba's hand cupped about it, rubbing it, before she did anything daring.

"Well, almost like yours," said Norie.

"Almost?"

"Well . . . " said Norie, comforting herself with the story-telling hum as she perched on the edge of Leora's bed.

Howie paced, agitated, two steps this way, two steps that.

"That one begins before the Rulers and the birmbas," Norie mused, swaying gently as if she were in the rocking chair.

Leora was grateful for the ordinariness of Norie telling her a story. But she almost cried, knowing it would be the last.

"It was back in the early days of the Dark Time," crooned Norie. "Your Grand Nan had a baby daughter. And right away she had a special silver locket made. A double locket, really. It was given to the child, but it was really meant, she said, for her daughter's daughter's daughter's daughters. Said it was to be separated into the two lockets for them, each with its own picture and words, when the time came. How'd she know there'd be two great-great-granddaughters? I don't know. Just like she knew there'd be a Disaster, I guess. On one locket was a picture of a sword, and on the other was a picture of a quill."

Leora, who had been clasping her locket, looked at it now. Shaped like a half-moon, it bore the delicately etched picture of a feather—a feather with the sharply angled point of a quill.

"Seems right—you getting the one with the quill, you with your gift for drawing and such," Norie continued.

"And what about the different words, Norie?"

" 'Who shall lead the land, Out of darkness into light,' "
Norie quoted. "The words went together, you see.
Which of them words is written on your locket there,
Leora?"

" 'Out of darkness into light,' it says. What does that
mean, Norie?"

"Bless me if I know. The Dark Time ended long ago,
and the sun's been shining ever since."

Norie fell silent.

Then, musing out loud, Leora said, "So Reba's locket
said, 'Who shall lead the land.' And had the sword on it.
What does it all mean?"

"Bless me if it ain't a mystery to me," Norie responded softly. "But how Reba loved that locket!"

"So this fellow," Howie interjected. "Had some weird
idea that this young lady . . . she might be a recruiter
or . . ."

"Howie! Shush!" Norie looked over her shoulder
nervously. Then she started, asking abruptly, "Did she
have red hair, Howie?"

"Well, the fellow didn't mention it. And soon as I
thought to ask, he'd up and left."

"Oh, Howie, d'you think she might have survived?"
Norie's eyes searched his face.

"Well," Howie considered. "Never found her bones,
did they? And besides," he said softly, meeting Leora's
eyes, "I never heard of anybody as was hurt by hoping."

Norie, looking now at Leora, moaned. "Oh, look at

us now! It does us no good getting our hopes all up. It's that big mouth of mine again. And yours, too, Howie. Hush now!"

"Well, Nor, if that mouth of yours can spare me some talkin' time, I could use you down in the kitchen for a spell. There's a course to plot, and there ain't any buoys. And two heads is better than one."

Clucking assurances of a prompt return, Norie followed Howie out of the room.

Leora enveloped the half-moon of silver in the soft webbing between her thumb and forefinger, encasing it as snugly as a seed in a winged pod.

What had become of the other half?

Flight

THE INSTITUTE. As Leora awoke in the night, the words hung about her, dark and heavy as stone.

But there had been other words circling in her dreams.

Never found her bones, did they?

Leora sat up. Who but Reba would be wearing a locket and asking after her? But Reba could not still be alive. Or could she?

A picture came to her—a picture from long ago—of Reba, crouching behind a laurel bush in a game of hide-and-seek, her hiding place given away by a shock of her wild red hair. Her hair had always made it hard for her to hide.

Suddenly Leora was out from under the covers, pulling on her shoes, and climbing into her clothes. She surprised herself with the speed of her decision. In the past few days she had surprised herself more than once.

On the rocker by her bed was an overstuffed knapsack. Norie must have come in after she was asleep and packed her a bag. For her trip to the Institute.

Well, she would take the bag. But not to the Institute. She would take it to Village Fifteen.

She pulled her great wool cape around herself. Like a turtle's shell, she thought, it would be her home. Before she left the room, she opened her bedside drawer and took out a picture she had drawn of a bird perched on a maple bough. She wrote *Norie* on it and left it on the little green rocker.

Then she was out the bedroom door. Through the window, she could see that the night sky was already breaking. She had little time to waste. From Norie's room came a soft snore. She tiptoed past and down the stairs.

The kitchen felt unfamiliar at this hour—silent, empty, waiting for the clatter and bustle of day. Leora found crusty loaves of bread, laid out for breakfast. Half of one fit tightly into one of her wide cape pockets. A generous hunk of cheese went into the other. Finally, she took down a soft leather flask, filled it from the water pitcher, and tied it around her waist.

The front hall, dark and close, still seemed inhabited by the ghosts of yesterday's confrontation. Stepping out of the front door, Leora felt welcomed by the sweet chill of the night air. She closed the door behind her.

Could this really be she, heading down the dark cobble streets of the village at dawn? Could this really be she, at the old gate again, heaving it open on creaking hinges? And passing through it—this time, not to return?

Forbidden, forbidden, the cold stone walls of the village whispered again at her back. But if anything, these voices propelled her forward. She did not slow her pace until she had left the voices behind.

It was the orchard that called her now, through early rhodora and scrubby spruce. As she came upon the clearing, it welcomed her with its sounds. The birds were celebrating the growing light with an assortment of songs—one sharp and boastful; one squeaky and insistent. And high in the trees, the lyrical plummeting call of the veery. Squirrels scampered out of her path, then held their ground, chattering and scolding, reminding her that this was *their* space.

She put down her knapsack and leaned up against the cool of the stone. She could not rest for long, of course. But for the moment, the orchard had received her as if it were home. At some other time she might have sat down with pen and paper and captured the beauty of it—the gnarled apple trees, the mosaic of newly leafing shrubs.

She tore off a hunk of bread, gnawing on it as she tried to focus her mind on her situation.

She had a limited amount of food and water.

She hadn't the vaguest idea which way to go.

And if she stayed here for very long, the guards were sure to find her.

She closed her eyes against the distractions of the orchard. Here in the open, away from the village, she felt free to expose her left hand. As if it might help her think, she put her webbed fingers tightly together and pressed them to her forehead. But all that came to her mind were pictures from the past: first a picture of her father and Reba in this very place—a sunny day, the trees heavy with summer growth; then the memory of her first sight of a birmba, tall and majestic in the rough shrubbery, just two days ago; and finally, an image of Wiggala—his wide eyes moving back and forth between her and the dense brush, as they waited for his mother.

She could almost feel Wiggala's wiry arms clinging possessively about her neck.

How had his mother known to come? Where to come? When to come?

"Oh, Wiggala."

The pictures in her imagination shifted into the present and became increasingly detailed. She could see the tiniest feathers of the birds she heard about her. And the veins of the tender leaves of the apple tree that murmured overhead. Then, quite improbably, she imagined the wind ruffling the glossy fur of Wiggala and his mother, standing in the brush, nearby.

She opened her eyes.

And there, not twenty paces away, in the growing light of day, they stood—Wiggala crouched expectantly, one paw resting on his mother's haunch.

"Wiggala!" she exclaimed.

The little creature pounced across the orchard in two leaps, and bounded into her arms.

"Wiggala," Leora gasped again, incredulous. Her left hand remembered the silky fur of Wiggala's neck, the softness of the little paw wound about her finger.

"I was wishing for you." Wiggala's tiny fingers explored her ear, stroking it as if it were the satin edge of a favorite blanket.

Leora locked eyes with the larger birmba, immobile at the orchard's edge. It was a waiting look, one that included her. It's time for you two children to come along, seemed to be the message.

Wiggala leaped to his mother's shoulder. Leora took in a deep breath of the orchard's mossy scent, and, with one last glance, captured the gnarled contours of the apple trees in her memory. Then she hoisted her sack, and followed.

～

With Wiggala riding piggyback, Mama Birmba slid smoothly and silently through the dense scrubby brush. It was a challenge to follow her, and Leora was glad there was no one about to hear the crackling of twigs and branches as she struggled to keep up.

Leora knew that the Edgeland was encircled by the Great Fence. With so much happening, she had not thought of it this morning. But as they emerged from a tight spread of fir saplings, there it was!

The fence was composed of closely placed spears, each taller than three men and each sharpened menacingly at the tip. The spiked barricade impaled the morning sky for as far as the eye could see.

But Mama Birmba did not even break her stride. She vanished with her passenger beneath a dense drooping cedar tree, only to reappear moments later on the far side of the barred enclosure.

Hating to be separated from the birmbas for even a moment, Leora dove beneath the boughs of the tree. The shelter of the lower branches revealed a broad ditch beneath the rusted base of the fence. Pushing her pack ahead of her, she scrambled through the damp passage to the safety, or dangers, of the far side.

Beyond the Great Fence

HERE IN THE FOREST stood spruce trees taller than she'd ever imagined. Nothing grew in their shadow but the moss, which accented the darkness with its iridescent green. The forest had a rich, piney smell, different from the orchard. Even the birdsong was new and unfamiliar.

The traveling was easier across this open forest floor of brown spruce needles, and as they moved more quickly, Leora grew increasingly confident that they would be safe from discovery by the guards. Her relief combined with her pleasure in the unfamiliar freedom and with her newfound hope that Reba might be alive.

The spruce trees were giving way to towering maples, the shadows of their tiny young leaves dancing in cheerful patches of sunlight. From time to time a winged maple seed would twirl down in her path, a special gift from the canopy above. She was sorry that she hadn't thought to put drawing paper in the pack that Norie had prepared for her.

It seemed to her they had been traveling for hours when at last the bobbing figure of the birmbas began to slow down. They had reached a sun-drenched opening in the trees, where wild strawberry blanketed the forest floor.

The little birmba seemed familiar with the stop, swinging eagerly down to earth and promptly disappearing. Leora heard him splashing before she even saw the little stream that wound through mossy banks.

Wiggala, who had been happily lapping the frigid water, watched in fascination as Leora drank from her soft leather flask and then immersed it in the stream. It bubbled noisily as it filled.

Approaching warily, he poked the bulging pouch. After a few pokes, he grew bolder and pinched it. The pouch made a "gubbley" sloshing sound that so amused him that he collapsed into what Leora soon realized was a birmba version of the giggles: a series of accelerating hiccups. Each new poke and slosh elicited a new cascade of hiccups, punctuated by a full somersault. Leora found all this so funny that soon she, too, was lost in giggles.

Eventually, their laughter was overtaken by hunger. Leora pulled her bread from one pocket and cheese from the other. She offered a piece of bread to Wiggala, but he shunned it in favor of something he found beneath the bushes: nitta berries!

Leora knew that nitta berries, as a mutant species, were poisonous to humans. But they were apparently not a problem for the birmbas. With a skill that could only come from long practice, Mama Birmba, too, was raking up the plentiful berries with her paw and devouring them by the mouthful.

Leora made a point of saving some bread and cheese for later. She did not want to think about what she would do when her food ran out.

Lying on her back with Wiggala happily planted on her chest, Leora watched as the little creature played with the shiny buckle of her knapsack. A cloud slid over the sun. The stroke of its shadow over their woodland clearing briefly called up her fears. She had a fleeting impression, at the corner of her eye, of a pair of eyes appearing in the brush. But when she looked, she saw nothing.

Mama Birmba had assumed an expectant stance. Wiggala reluctantly let go of Leora's brass buckle. It was time to move on.

Leora gave their stopping place a farewell look. Someday she would draw this, too. Then she turned and followed the birmbas back into the shadows of the woods.

∾

She hardly noticed their surroundings as they continued on their journey. Her enchantment with her new world had given way to worries and to questions that circled without answers.

The day's light had begun to fade. Mama Birmba stopped, once again, beside a bubbling brook. The site was commanded by a towering cedar, its outer foliage drooping almost to the ground. Wiggala entered and exited the dense cedar as if it were home.

From somewhere, Mama Birmba produced a pyramid of barka nuts, along with an assortment of mushrooms. Although Leora was aware that some mushrooms were edible, she knew that barka nuts, coming from the mutant barka tree, were as poisonous to humans as nitta berries.

Exhausted from the long day's travel, Leora settled down and leaned against a maple trunk. Wiggala took advantage of her position, climbed on her shoulder, and began checking her hair for fleas, occasionally pretending to catch one. Leora was comforted by the feeling of the tiny fingers tugging softly on her hair, parting it, exploring her scalp. All the while, she stroked Wiggala's long toes with the tips of her webbed fingers.

It was as they sat like this that she became aware of an addition to their company. Had she heard a low growl? Or had she simply felt it in her bones? There, half crouched at the edge of the cedar tree, was *another birmba!*

Much larger than Wiggala, but not as large as Mama

Birmba. Down one shoulder and upper arm it bore a ragged scar of pale fur. Its narrowed eyes bored into her, and a curl of its lip showed the teeth below.

If it had not been for Wiggala's fingers continuing their rhythmic play in her hair, and for Mama Birmba's disinterested stance, Leora would have assumed that this new arrival was an enemy. But their obvious familiarity with him told her that this was a member of the family. She suspected that the angry eyes now locked with her own belonged to Wiggala's older brother.

Through the rest of that evening Leora avoided looking directly at this unfriendly creature, but she never took her attention off him. And the same, she thought, was true of the beast himself. He paced the area restlessly, even as he helped himself to the barka nuts and mushrooms, rarely looking at her directly, but radiating hostility.

Eventually, as Leora ate her bread and cheese, her heart stopped pounding. With Mama Birmba and Wiggala nearby, she couldn't help but feel safe.

Mama Birmba was roaming the low brush gathering long lengths of calpa vines and disappearing from time to time into the heart of the cedar tree.

Finally, Wiggala planted himself at an opening in the tree's flat-needled walls and looked at Leora with waiting eyes. She was expected within.

Relieved to see that Wiggala's older brother had stationed himself at the base of a distant tree, Leora lifted her pack and entered the tree's enclosure. A multitude of slender branches radiated from the trunk at head height, then drooped almost to the ground, providing an ample and welcoming space within. The base of the trunk was immense but quickly divided into a dozen or more smaller but substantial trunks that rose in a widening cone.

Wiggala scrambled up one of these trunks, looking back at Leora. As her eyes became accustomed to the darkness, she made out two adjacent shapes suspended in the center of the tree. They looked something like hammocks, roughly woven from vines.

Mama Birmba settled herself in the larger of these, and, as Leora watched, Wiggala scampered up and nestled against his mother's body. Leora knew the other hammock must be for her!

As her fingers and toes sought branch stubs for support, the great cedar, rustling in the breeze, welcomed her with its sweet rough skin and its many strong arms.

When at last she slid into her spot, tucking her cape about her, she was so close to Wiggala she could hear his soft breath and look into his shining night eyes.

"Good-night, Wiggala," she whispered, and within minutes she was fast asleep, dreaming that she was inside a translucent eggshell in her very own bird's nest.

The Path Begins

LEORA WOKE to the rat-a-tat of a woodpecker. From her nest she could see the morning sun illuminating the budding red maple, the leaves still furled as tightly as berries. A movement above drew her eye to the bushy tails of two red squirrels in a game of chase through the slender upper branches.

Through half-open eyes she watched Mama Birmba groom Wiggala in the adjoining nest, parting the shiny fur with her long fingers, scratching, rubbing. Wiggala scrambled out of Mama's lap, and, in one quick pounce, landed on Leora's belly. With eager eyes and fingers he proceeded to explore the molded metal button of her cape.

He wriggled with pleasure as she massaged the base of his neck. She stroked the pink skin of his furless palm, causing his little fingers to open and close around her own. It was funny that her webbed hand seemed to know exactly how to pet this little bundle of animal.

The distant sound of a crow put Wiggala and Mama Birmba on the alert. Instinctively, Leora followed their example and froze.

Back and forth the crows cawed to each other, their calls growing closer and closer. Leora heard the distant sound of crackling branches. Would any forest animal move so loudly and carelessly?

Then the rattle of metal. Guards! She wanted to peek out of the nest, but dared not. Along with Wiggala and Mama Birmba, she barely breathed.

"Fan out and search!" Leora heard the order barked at top volume.

"Fan out and search!" the order was echoed. "And keep your eyes open. This will be the last search before we head east."

Leora heard the stomping and crunching of feet as they spread out in different directions. They were searching for her! Her heart pounded so hard she thought that Wiggala, motionless on her chest, must be able to feel it. With her webbed hand still on Wiggala's shoulder, she and the birmba had melded together into a single wary being.

"So where will it be next, sir?" The voice was almost directly beneath her.

"We'll head east toward the sea, then down to Village Fifteen."

Leora thought that she recognized the voices of the captain and his lieutenant.

"Village Fifteen, sir?"

"Village Fifteen. There's word that it's at the center of some rebel activity."

"Indeed!"

"They're recruiting there," the captain's voice continued. "We were alerted a while back about one of their recruiters. We don't know who she is or where she comes from. Probably sent from outside Maynor to make trouble for us."

"A woman?" the lieutenant said with surprise.

"A young woman, they say."

"Should be easy to capture."

"Capture? We may do that in the end. But the first plan is to let her recruit one of our own. We'll let her betray her own cause before we take her prisoner."

The lieutenant laughed. "Put a spy in their midst. Clever, I'd say."

The gradual approach of more breaking brush told Leora that the men were returning from their search.

"Collect them," said the captain to the lieutenant. "We're wasting our time here."

"Sir," came a new voice. Leora's skin prickled. Wilfert!

"Excuse . . . sir . . . Pardon the liberty . . . sir," came that familiar voice. "Ought we not . . . shouldn't we look till we find her. Sir?"

"If the birmbas haven't already got her, she'll die of hunger, Blencher. We have bigger fish to fry."

Despite the dismissal, the wheedling persisted.

"Just another few hours . . . sir . . . I'll stay behind . . . and find her myself."

There was a pause. Was the captain considering it?

But he only barked, "I gave the order to move on, Blencher."

"Collect troops! Forward!"

Leora did not allow herself to take a deep breath until the sounds of the troops were gone. She felt Wiggala, too, relaxing beneath her hand, growing heavy on her chest. But she followed the birmbas' lead and remained motionless.

This was the second time Leora had heard of *rebel activity*, both times in conjunction with *recruiting*. Now that she thought of it, Howie had mentioned *recruiting*, too. Could the young woman the guards spoke of be the same person Howie's friend had seen? Could it be Reba? Was she a *rebel*?

Leora had a clear memory of her sister at play, her right hand holding a staff as she parried imaginary blows and charged imaginary opponents. She had always been a fighter. "Fierce as a tiger," their father had called her.

The captain's words rang in her ears: . . . recruit one of our own . . . betray her own cause . . . then take her.

"Oh, Reba." She sighed, fingering her locket.

She did not entirely understand what was going on, but if Reba was alive, and was one of the rebels, Leora must find her and warn her.

Wiggala, having failed to tug off Leora's coveted cape button, rediscovered her knapsack buckle and looked into her eyes beseechingly, like a child begging for a toy. This, too, having failed, he catapulted nimbly to his mother's shoulders and piggybacked a free ride out of the nest and down to the ground.

Leora sat up and took a last look around, committing to memory the patterns of this newly leafing world from her special perch.

By the time she had made her way to the bottom of the tree, the birmbas were collecting a breakfast of barka nuts and nitta berries and bits of a white rootlike thing. While Wiggala and Mama Birmba foraged, Leora went to the stream's edge.

She had a decision to make.

If there was any chance at all that Reba was alive, Leora had to get to Village Fifteen and warn her. And wherever Village Fifteen was, it was no place for a birmba.

The time had come to say good-bye to her new friends.

She filled her pouch with water as quietly as she could. Under the circumstances, this was not the moment for a bout of giggles with Wiggala.

When Leora returned to the clearing, Wiggala leaped

eagerly onto her back, combing his busy fingers through her hair.

"Oh, Wiggala," Leora said sadly. "I have to go."

There. She had said it. But could she do it?

Leora's eyes met Mama Birmba's. It was a long and steady gaze. She could feel herself gathering courage from something in those eyes. She reached upward, stroking Wiggala's neck with her webbed hand. Little fingers curled tightly around her own.

"I have to go, Wiggala," she said again. "I have to warn my sister."

But she made no move to detach her fingers from her little friend's grip.

"Next time I see you," Leora said, as if it were Wiggala who still needed convincing, "I'll give you a whole bagful of buckles and buttons and shiny things."

It was then that Mama Birmba, in two slow steps, arrived at her side, gently detached Wiggala's fingers from Leora's webbed hand, and swooped up her protesting offspring. Did Mama Birmba understand that Leora had business to attend to? Was it deliberate the way her softly furred fingers gave one quick stroke to Leora's left hand?

Intentional or no, Leora took comfort and strength from it. Just enough to help her hold her ground as Mama Birmba, after one last gaze, melted silently into the cover of the high brush with a mournful-eyed Wiggala, leaving Leora standing alone in the glade.

Surprise Encounter

LEORA did not have long to worry about finding the way. Having followed the sun's invitation toward a clearing in the shrubs, she found herself, to her surprise, on a narrow but well-frequented path. The guardsmen's path!

East toward the sea, then down to Village Fifteen, they had said. She could not be sure it went to Village Fifteen, but judging from the direction of the rising sun, it did head roughly east.

The ground, still touched by nighttime frost, was crisp but spongy under its blanket of dried leaves. It made her nervous to use the same path as the guards. She would have to be careful.

At first she steered clear of the new-species plants along the trail. If it ends in "a," stay away, she had learned at school. But remembering the sight of the birmbas eating barka nuts and nitta berries, she found herself looking at these plants with a new eye.

If you didn't think of it as poisonous, the barka tree was a thing of beauty. Its foliage, so fine, lit up the woods in little puffs of bright green haze wherever it was struck by the low morning sun. The barka nuts grew in abundance on the trunk itself, almost indistinguishable from the deeply furrowed bark in which they were embedded.

The deep purple nitta berries, hidden in the shade of larger bushes, were less visible. But she could imagine how they must cheer the late-winter landscape with their purply pink blossoms.

As she walked she imagined that she had found Reba and was drawing pictures for her of this . . . and this . . . and this.

It seemed no time at all before Leora noticed that the sun was high in the sky. She found herself a spot in a clearing just off the path, and opened her pack for the first time.

She knew Norie well enough to be certain that her bag would be well stocked with snacks—snacks for her trip to the Institute. She was not disappointed. Wrapped in a clean white dishcloth she found an assortment of crusty pastries.

Berry tarts had never tasted so good. She forced herself to eat them slowly, savoring each morsel of the flaky crust and smooth sweet filling.

But she'd better save the rest for later. She rolled them back up reluctantly and settled for an apple. It helped to quench her thirst. She'd already drunk most of the water in her pouch. She'd have to find more soon.

A rustling of leaves alarmed her, but a movement in the ferns revealed nothing more than a tiny red squirrel scampering toward the base of a great maple.

"You're as noisy as an elephant, little squirrel," Leora said in relief.

So far, each time she had been startled by a sound in the brush, the culprit had turned out to be the tiniest of animals. But she was finding it increasingly hard to shake an apprehension that there was something much larger out there than a squirrel.

For the moment, however, she felt reassured. Her morning's efforts had left her tired, and she leaned now against the cool trunk of the maple.

A break in the clouds brought a shaft of light, brightening the tops of the distant spruce, then widening to include her in its warm beam.

She spread out the fingers of her left hand. The warmth of the sun felt unfamiliar on the delicate webbing between her fingers. As she dozed off, she dreamed that she was a dragonfly, freshly hatched, drying its wings in the noonday sun.

~

Leora awoke with a start. The landscape of the glade had been changed again—this time by the disappearance of the sun behind a shield of lowering gray. The sweet spell of the morning was gone. She felt cold and disoriented.

A dream she couldn't quite remember haunted her and filled her with dread.

Was there someone, something, out there?

With a new sense of urgency, she tightened the straps on her pack and left the glade for the rough path. But was it wise to travel on this well-worn path? She might easily stumble upon the guardsmen as she moved forward. Or be surprised by them from behind.

She willed herself to hurry, but her progress through the brush became increasingly difficult. This morning's hope and energy had disappeared. She was thirsty. Her muscles ached. How many more minutes, hours, and days would be like this? And how could she have fooled herself into thinking that there was any hope that Reba could be alive?

Maybe she should just sit in the middle of the path and let the guards find her. At least at the Institute she would have food and water and a place to sleep.

But it took only a minute to remember that Wilfert himself was a guardsman now. She imagined that it would be he who would grab her and bind her hands. She could almost feel the pressure of his fingers on her wrists.

And if Reba *was* alive, she, too, was in danger.

No, this was no time to give up.

Suddenly, Leora froze.

Without warning, a shadow had fallen over the path. The shadow was not attached to a guard.

It was attached to the looming form of a birmba!

With the large creature only three yards away, all her old school lessons about the beasts' ferocity came flooding back to her. Violent, blood-thirsty, man-eating beasts. They had killed her father. They could surely kill her.

In the next second, however, the ragged pale fur on the creature's shoulder brought recognition. It was Wiggala's older brother!

Even without the scarred patch on his shoulder, she would have easily recognized the belligerence of that gaze. Her body tensed for flight.

If the creature meant well, it would get out of her way.

It did not.

If it intended her harm, it could leap on her in a single bound.

It did not.

Why was he here?

Inching backward, she came into firm contact with the solid trunk of a tree. If she wanted to put more space between herself and him, she could only run. But could she run fast enough? Her eyes locked with his. She stood with her back glued to the tree for what seemed like an eternity.

It was then that she heard something, much louder than her own pounding chest. Not fifty yards ahead, it was the sound of a human voice!

She couldn't make out the words, but the tone was rough, impatient. Now a second voice, followed by the rattling of metal.

Guardsmen, gathering up their arms! Perhaps they were the same guards she had overheard that very morning.

Another few minutes forward, and she would have stumbled into their midst.

Which was worse: the guards or the birmba?

Out of the frying pan, into the fire, she could hear Norie's voice saying.

But which was the frying pan and which the fire? she wondered.

Still and quiet as a woodland creature in danger, she looked at the animal before her. Although its eyes were fixed on Leora, she could tell that its attention, too, was on the sounds in the woods beyond.

It was as if the beast were waiting for the guardsmen to be out of earshot so he could attack her.

The sound of voices and the muffled clatter of metal seemed to be retreating. But it was not too late to call for help.

As if divining her thought, the shaggy form before her dropped suddenly and softly to its haunches, turning its head casually away, its ferocity melted.

Although she knew it was her last chance to cry out and be heard, the balance had tipped. She would let the moment pass.

As minutes went by, the creature before her maintained his semblance of bored innocence. He scratched at the earth with his finely furred fingers and popped something into his mouth.

He had found a nest of rakina bugs. And he was eating them! Leora's fear was replaced by squeamish surprise. If she ever saw Howie again she would have to tell him about it.

She wondered if Wiggala ate bugs, too. She sighed, and reminded herself that this beast in front of her was, after all, Wiggala's brother. How bad could he be?

"You're just a *grumpy bear*," she said crossly, mostly to reassure herself.

He looked at her and glowered. But she was no longer alarmed.

It certainly had been a lucky coincidence, his stepping in her path just in time to prevent her from meeting up with the guards.

Still, she wondered, why *was* he here? Had he actually followed her?

"Well, you've satisfied your curiosity, and scared the wits out of me," she said out loud, her fear having dissolved into an uncharacteristic feeling of impatience. "You can get out of my way and go home."

The creature seemed to understand. He rose slowly

from his haunches, ambled out of the path, and gazed off into the woods. She was clearly free to move on.

He no longer looked as enormous to her as he had when she was frightened of him. When he looked directly at her, his eyes were narrowed and suspicious. But when he looked away from her, as he did now, his eyes were large and soft. Like Wiggala's.

Well, she didn't know what his problem was. But she had no time to waste.

She adjusted the straps on her pack, turned her back on the beast, and, moving as quickly as she dared, left him behind.

Company

HER NEAR MISS with the guards at least assured her that she was on the right path. But she would have to concentrate on moving more silently. She made each step consciously now, avoiding the rustling of dry leaves, the snapping of twigs.

She couldn't get the picture of the birmba out of her mind. Nor could she shake an impression of . . . was it hurt? . . . in those large eyes. She was sorry she'd left him so rudely. Even if he was just an animal, she could have said good-bye.

Leora didn't think her journey could get more difficult, but it did. She hadn't known she could feel this thirsty. Or hungry. The path had grown rougher. Often she found her way blocked by fallen trees, some of them too large to climb over. As she worked her way around these larger ones, she had trouble finding the path again.

Most of all, there was the problem of her hand. Seldom used, it was weak, and the muscles in her forearm ached from the effort it took to make her way through the forest. Moreover, the webbing between her fingers was delicate. Confronted with an enormous fallen spruce, she steadied herself with her right hand and tried to break an obstructing branch with her left. She failed, scratching the web between her thumb and forefinger in the process. She had never hurt it before. It bled profusely.

"Stupid hand!" she said out loud.

At this rate she would never find Reba, much less save her.

Working her way around the fallen tree, she scratched herself repeatedly in the struggle through heavy underbrush.

Finally she had to admit that the task was simply beyond her. She had no hope of finding Reba. No hope of saving Reba. It was a fact.

"Stupid frog paw!"

She thought about the Institute, where Tanette and her stepmother and Wilfert said that she belonged.

By the time she stumbled into a clearing, Leora's vision was clouded with tears. She made out the profusion of white bunchberry blossoms that carpeted the forest floor, but it wasn't until she wiped the tears from her eyes that she distinguished a massive dark form, all but invisible in the shadow of a great maple trunk.

It was Wiggala's brother! Again!

The last thing she would have expected herself to do under the circumstances was to laugh. But that is what she did.

"Well, it's a good thing I didn't say 'good-bye' to you," she said. She noted with surprise that it was sort of an attempt at a joke. She had never made a joke before, and she wasn't sure that it was a very good one. Especially after the way she'd left him.

The beast scowled at her with his familiar narrowed eyes.

She still didn't know why he was here, but it was now clear that his presence was no accident. Whatever the reason, she was grateful for his company. She plunked herself down on a low lichened trunk.

"Well, I don't know about you, but I could drink a river," Leora said. She opened her pack and upturned her leather water bag over her mouth, hoping vainly for a few last drops.

She had no sooner tossed it to the ground than the birmba swooped it up with his great hand-paw and loped off into the woods. Leora stared, stunned, in the direction of his retreat.

Where was he going? Why had he taken the bag? What would she do without it? The questions were still swirling in her mind when the crackling of branches signaled his return. With bag still in hand, she was glad to see.

And now he offered it back to her. Still puzzled, she accepted the return of the leather pouch with relief. Unprepared for its weight, she almost dropped it.

"Water!" Leora laughed. The bag was cool and heavy and damp.

"I'm *very* glad I didn't say good-bye to you," she said. As an afterthought, she added, "That was a joke."

The water was cool and delicious, and she drank her fill.

It would be silly to offer him the bag, so she unwrapped her pastries from their dishcloth and offered him a berry tart. Leora could see his nostrils flare as he assessed the peace offering. Although he made no move toward her, his eyes remained glued to the pastry, and his nose continued to work. At the very least, he was curious.

"Please!" she said, extending it farther.

He reached for it gingerly, taking cautious hold of it as if it were an oversized and mysterious bug.

"It won't bite you," Leora said, breaking off a morsel of one of the remaining tarts. He watched as she put it into her mouth and chewed. He turned his own tart over and over, flared his nostrils, and at last popped the whole thing into his mouth as if it were no bigger than a rakina bug.

There was no misinterpreting the speed with which

his eyes shot to the remaining tart. She didn't have the heart to deny him and handed it over quickly, knowing that if she thought about it for long she might not be so generous.

He hesitated, as if aware that he would be depriving her of it, but he was clearly unable to resist. Better than bugs, Leora thought, smiling, as she watched the tart disappear in a gulp.

The animal turned carelessly, and, running his paw down the rough barka trunk, dislodged a collection of shiny barka nuts.

It was his turn to extend one to Leora.

Leora hesitated. If it ends in "a," stay away.

Everyone knew that mutant plants were poisonous. But she had seen Wiggala and Mama Birmba eating the nuts the night before. How could it be safe for them and not for her?

The animal was putting one into his mouth, chewing deliberately, almost as if to demonstrate its safety.

Maybe it was a reluctance to be rude to him a second time. Maybe it was the fear that sooner or later hunger would make her too weak to proceed if she didn't take the chance. She reached for it. She explored its fissured surface with her webbed hand. Something in the feel of it, something she could not have described, told her she had nothing to fear.

Nibble by nibble, she ate her first barka nut. An odd taste. But sweet, with a texture almost like a chestnut.

Many barka nuts later, Leora leaned back against a tree trunk, pleasantly full. Out of the corner of her eye, she observed her companion, crouched now beside her. If his look was no longer hostile, it was still highly suspicious. His eyes still narrowed when he looked at her.

Leora had never much wondered before how she appeared to others. She had always assumed that people in the village, if they saw her at all, simply saw her as defective. She found herself wondering now what it was that this creature saw when he looked at her. Was he particularly suspicious of *her*? Or did he just hate people?

Leora put her webbed hand on the rough fur of his forearm, and before she knew that the question was in her mind, it popped out of her mouth. "Where's *your* father?"

The creature, of course, could not answer her. But in that instant, an understanding came to her as surely and clearly as if it had been spoken.

"He was killed by the guards, wasn't he?" she said.

He turned his massive head and looked at her. This time, his eyes stayed large and soft.

"You know what I'm beginning to think?" she went on, unaware that her webbed fingers still rested on the creature's arm. "I'm beginning to think it was the guards who killed my father, too."

Between them, for some minutes, there was a silence.

"Tomo," she said, at first in her mind, and then softly, out loud. "I'll call you Tomo."

As if in acceptance of this name, the creature turned again and looked at her. He looked her straight in the eye, a long and steady gaze. Something in that look was deep and old and beyond things she could know with her mind. It was in a language only her hand could begin to understand.

~

Darkness stole quickly over the flower-carpeted clearing. Leora watched curiously as Tomo foraged for vines and wove them into a hammocklike nest. She was fairly sure that he had not spent the night before in a nest but curled up beneath the shrubbery. It became apparent, at last, that the nest was intended for her.

"You were sent to take care of me, weren't you?" Leora said. "You stopped me from walking into the guards."

Tomo looked as if he'd fallen victim to a sudden distracting attack of fleabites.

"Thank you," she said. Tomo scratched again, as if one particular fleabite required a great deal of attention indeed.

Struggling up the tree trunk, she thought he must have taken some pains to choose one that she would be able to climb at all. Not until she was settled in her nest did she see him circle the clearing and choose a spot to curl up for the night.

She snuggled into her roughly twined bed. The stars winked on and off as wispy clouds raced across the sky. She remembered the feeling of Tomo's coarse fur as she rested her webbed hand upon it.

Had it been a coincidence that it was then that he had come to trust her? And a coincidence that Wiggala had become friendly the moment she extended her webbed fingers through the bars in the basement cage?

Thoughtfully, with her right hand, she massaged the soft skin of her left.

In her dream that night, Wilfert smiled a thin smile and beckoned across a narrow alleyway to an unsuspecting Reba. Reba approached him with hand outstretched.

Planted firmly in Reba's path, striving mightily to intercept the encounter, was a tiny web-footed frog.

More Company

THE FOLLOWING DAY brought a deep blue sky and a light breeze. It carried no hint of the surprise to come.

After Leora and Tomo shared a breakfast of nitta berries and calpa root, she filled up her drinking flask. It seemed to be understood that Tomo would accompany her.

For the most part, she kept to the path, though she noticed that Tomo seemed to avoid it as much as possible, traveling parallel with her in the near brush.

She felt less inclined to chatter with Tomo than she did with the birds and squirrels, but the silence between them seemed to hold a deep level of understanding. Intuitively, he anticipated each of her needs, whether for food, water, or rest.

They had stopped in a thicket of young aspen trees. Leora was tired and would have liked to rest a little longer beneath the rustle of the silver-lined leaves. But Tomo had become restless and was making nervous forays into the deeper brush, now this way, now that. What was he so anxious about?

Leora knew he would be back again shortly, and impatient to move along. So she tied her water bag about her waist and arranged the straps of her knapsack.

It was as she hoisted her pack that it happened.

With no more warning than the sound of two crashing footsteps, a hand was clapped over her mouth from behind. She found herself hoisted roughly off her feet and trundled off through a blur of underbrush.

Through her mind flashed pictures of Norie and Howie; of Reba, whom she would never get a chance to warn; of Tomo, Wiggala, and Mama Birmba.

Terror mingled with confusion. How had a guard managed to sneak up on her so quietly? Would he deliver her to the Institute? Or would he kill her?

At last he stopped and plunked her down. She could hear him gasping for breath as he spun her around, a hand still on her mouth, whispering, "Don't make a sound!"

Her mind registered the familiar accent before she even saw the face. She was looking into the anxious brown eyes of *Howie*!

"Don't make a sound, now," he said, removing his hand from her mouth. "I just spied a birmba not two minutes from here. I was afraid you'd cry out when you spotted me and give us away. We don't want to be a birmba's dinner, do we? But," he added quickly, "don't you worry; we'll come out of this well enough. I've got my trusty brush-whacker here," he finished, patting the leather sheath at his belt. "And I know how to use it!"

Amazement had tied Leora's tongue, but now she threw her arms around him. It was hard to say which of them was more surprised by the gesture. But he was not displeased. And Leora was growing used to surprising herself these days.

"Howie!" she exclaimed.

"Shhhhhh, Leora!" he said, making a move to cover her mouth again.

Leora began to explain to him, in a whisper, why there was no need to whisper.

"That was my friend you saw," she protested. "He's not dangerous!"

"Friend?" Howie asked. "I saw nobody. Only a birmba. Not full grown perhaps, but big enough. And if you're with someone, why, they're in danger, too!"

"I mean the *birmba*, Howie. *He's* my friend! Howie, you'll never believe this," she said, her voice getting louder in her excitement.

"Shhhhhh." Howie put his hand over her mouth again.

And as they stood there, Tomo charged out of the brush with a snarl, a growl, and teeth bared for battle.

"Holy, holy!" gasped Howie, reaching for his knife.

"Get behind me, Leora." He pulled his long blade out of its scabbard.

"Stop!" Leora yelled. "Howie! He's my friend. He's not like you think."

"Get behind me, Leora!" Howie yelled again. "He'll kill you!"

"You'll kill *each other*! For no reason!"

But Howie's blade was angling for action, and she knew she could not make him understand. She turned her attention to Tomo.

"Tomo. Stop! He's my friend. He was only trying to protect me." But her words had no effect. Tomo had moved closer, rolling his head and gnashing his teeth. *This* was the kind of birmba depicted in the pictures at school!

There was only one chance. Leora put her webbed hand swiftly on Tomo's shoulder. "He's not one of the guards, Tomo. He's a friend."

The effect was instantaneous. Tomo lowered his menacing paw. His eyes were still narrowed, and he did not back down. But the threat was obviously gone.

"Well, I'll be . . . Now how'd you do that?" Howie asked. He continued to hold his knife at the ready while he marveled. "Took the wind right out of his sails, you did. Never saw the like."

"Well . . ." Leora began. And as Tomo paced suspiciously nearby, Leora tried as best she could to tell Howie of her last two days. She told about Wiggala and

Mama Birmba and Tomo; about nitta berries and barka nuts; about nests made of calpa vines; about overhearing the guards and how Tomo had saved her from meeting up with them later on.

Throughout, Howie, glancing with widening eyes at the restless beast, only interrupted to exclaim, "Well, blow me down," and "I'll be scuttled." And finally, when all was told, "Well, if it weren't you telling me, and I didn't see the critter here with my own eyes, I'd've said that tale was taller than a tops'l."

Leora could see that Howie was also surprised at her talking so much. For the first time it dawned on her how very quiet she had always been.

She had omitted the things that she couldn't be sure of—such as her growing suspicion that thoughts could flow through her hand: both to, and from, the birmbas. And her conjecture that Tomo's father, and perhaps her own, had been killed by guards.

Then it was Howie's turn to fill Leora in on all that had passed since she left.

"Well, Norie, you can imagine, once she laid eyes on your empty bunk, and saw the pack gone—well, she knew you'd flown the coop. You'd've thought the heavens had opened up. The tears that woman shed! All she could say was, if only she'd've packed you more food . . .

"I'll confess I was ready to walk off the plank m'self. Nor and I had decided the night before I'd get you out of there before morning. Who'd have thought you'd beat me to it! You must've left at pitch dark.

"A regular hurricane, it was. Lady Blencher half hysterical—feeling guilty, if you ask me. And Tanette all pale. And quiet, if you'd believe that. All of us figuring you'd be eaten by the birmbas, or starve to death. Who'd've guessed it was the *birmbas* were feeding *you*.

"And his *lordship* Wilfert, in one of those silent evil spells of his—losing two precious prisoners in as many days.

"And Norie, she couldn't get me out of there fast enough to look for you—as if I hadn't set my rudder that way already. Me, a tracker, and it took me this long to pick up your trail!"

"Howie. Won't the guards miss you?"

"And what if they do? Though most like they pushed off to look for you thinking I was about the village somewhere. There's choppers enough without me. No, I doubt they'll have missed me.

"But, Leora. I don't want you setting too much hope on finding Reba. It's a thin chance she's alive. And if she is, it's a thinner chance you'll find her."

"I have to try, Howie."

"Well, then. To Village Fifteen it is," Howie said without pause. "But there's troops expected in both directions along this path. We'll sight a safer course in the backwoods. It'll be harder going, but I've got a compass, and I sharpened my brush-whacker before I left."

Travel was indeed slower, as Howie hacked his way through the denser spots. With Howie there, Tomo disappeared for long periods of time, ambling unexpectedly back onto their track from time to time. Leora was always relieved when he reappeared. But she could see that Howie was still nervous around him, referring to him as *that varmint*.

When at last they stopped for a midafternoon rest, Leora got her wish—for Howie to see with his own eyes how she and Tomo ate nitta berries and barka nuts.

"Well, I'll be hoisted," he exclaimed with satisfactory amazement. "Tell me you'll be eating the brass fittings next."

She felt as if she were holding her first tea party.

She was only sorry her guests treated each other like enemies.

Leora Leads the Way

"Which bird do you think has the most beautiful song, Howie?" A darkening of the sky had encouraged a chorus of excited twittering in the forest around them.

"Well, I like the veery, myself. But folks say the sweetest song of all was the hermit thrush."

"The hermit thrush? Why do they call it a hermit thrush?"

"It's a shy little thing. You'll hardly ever see it," he said. "I've never even heard it myself. In fact no one alive has heard it. It stopped singing long ago."

"Why?"

"Well . . . the story goes that it had such a beautiful song that one of the first Rulers of Maynor had one captured. He put it in a cage. As if you could own a bird or its song." Howie looked over his shoulder and lowered his voice.

"Poor thing died in a day. Ever since then, no one has heard a hermit thrush sing. But my grandmother said it was the sweetest sound. 'Like a waterfall going backward,' she used to say."

There was something familiar about the story. Yes, she was sure of it. Their father had told it to her and Reba. In the orchard. She remembered how the story had upset her, and how Reba had comforted her, assuring her that the bird would not be silent forever.

"Will it ever sing again?" she asked now.

"Not so long as the Rulers rule, folks say," said Howie, looking up nervously at the darkening sky. "And that'll be forever. So when you hear folks say, 'Not till the hermit thrush sings,' what they're really saying is 'never.' "

"But the rebels are against the Rulers!" Leora cried, her thoughts turning to Reba.

"The rebels are against the Rulers, all right. But they haven't the chance of a whippoorwill in a hurricane. No, Leora, you and I . . . we'll never hear that song."

A rumble of distant thunder brought Howie to his feet. "There's some heavy weather blowing in from the east. If I plot the course right and we make good headway, there's a place we can find shelter."

"Not a village?" Leora asked, following Howie into the darkening woods.

"Yes and no. It's what they call a ghost town—what's left of a village from the Before Time. All burned down and overgrown mostly—foundations and old cellars and what. But there's one big old building—made of solid mortar—where there's enough left to keep a body almost dry."

The wind was rising, the trees picking up its force in a whiffling roar. It made Leora feel small, like a tiny forest creature scurrying in the leaves.

Tomo was nowhere in sight. Howie, hurrying to beat the storm, had stopped to wait for her. She found him considering their path.

"I've never approached the place from this neck of the woods before. The first stickler is to figure our way to a big stretch of cedar forest that lies just to the west of the town. From there it'll take some fancy figuring and some luck to steer our way to the town itself. So . . . which way will it be," he asked himself out loud. "Over the knoll, or along the bank of the stream?"

"It must be that way," she said tentatively. She stared at her webbed hand, which was pointing along the edge of the brook.

"Your flip of the coin's as good as mine," Howie said, proceeding along the water's edge.

"Well, you charted it just right, Leora," Howie said, as they came in sight of a majestic stretch of cedar trees. "Unfortunately, the next call's even harder. A little too far this way or that and we'll miss the place altogether. And I don't much like the look of things."

The cedars stood in dark relief against an angry gray

sky, and the wind gusted with such force that Leora caught on to a nearby sapling to steady herself.

"It's that way." This time she spoke with conviction, her hand pointing straight into the wind.

Howie looked back and forth from her hand to her face, turning something over in his mind as he did so.

"How 'bout I follow *you*," he said thoughtfully. "I'm not familiar with these waters myself. You brought us here on target, didn't you? You might as well take a turn at the helm."

Leora caught him casting another odd look at her as she assumed the lead. Fortunately, the passage was easier here, the cedars were well spaced, and little else grew in the forest to impede their travel. Before long, she was threading her way through the forest as surely as if she were walking a well-trodden path.

Leora realized now that they had not seen Tomo for some time. Thinking about him as she forged ahead, leaning into the wind, she was surprised to realize how fond she had grown of him. She was fond of Howie, too. She thought sadly that it seemed unlikely that Tomo and Howie would ever be very comfortable with each other.

"Well, I'll be a whale's elbow," she heard Howie exclaim as they emerged from the cedars into an expanse of more open terrain. "Thar she blows, Leora." He was pointing at the gray remains of an ancient structure. "You navigate better 'n a bird dog," he said with a chuckle. "Keep it a secret now. Or the guards'll have you scouting track faster than a weasel spits."

Suddenly the sky was split by a ragged stick of lightning and the downpour was upon them.

"Run, Leora!" Howie yelled, and they raced through the blinding sheet of water toward the crumbled building.

As they got closer, Leora noticed the words TOWN HALL engraved in the lintel over the door. She scrambled up the stone stairs and into the dark interior.

"As dark as a tomb. And it could do with some caulking." Howie's voice echoed off the empty walls.

Leora explored the great hall with fascination. She had never been in a building from the Before Time. There were few of them left standing in Maynor. Howie said it was because most of the buildings before the Disaster had been made of wood and got burned in the great fires.

She ran her hand over the stone wall and stroked the wide sill of the window openings. Their shelter leaked, but she felt cozy, watching the descent of night through the pounding rain. Beneath the dark ceiling of the storm, over a distant ridge of night-dark trees, a fattening moon was struggling through a cloud break.

"It'll be clear tomorrow," Howie said, pointing at it. "But if it gets much wetter in here, we'll have to lower the lifeboats. There's another two rooms beyond this one. The last's the driest."

"But how will Tomo find us?"

"Don't worry about him, Leora. Varmints. They might be dumb, but where smell's concerned, they can't be beat. He'll find us with his nose."

Leora hoped that was so.

The second room, missing much of its roof, was even wetter than the first. But the third and last, small and windowless, was relatively tight.

Howie rummaged in his pack, which seemed to hold "everything but the parson's pulpit," as Norie liked to say. Soon they had a little candle glowing on a stone bench. Their shelter from the storm promised to be a comfortable one. But where was Tomo?

Leora's hand gave a flutter like a bird in danger. She wrapped her cape tightly around herself and moved closer to the candle.

Town Hall

"WHY IS IT called 'Town Hall,' Howie?" Leora asked, once they had made themselves as comfortable as possible. "What do you think they used this building for? Was this the Rulers' fort?"

"Well, it's told that in the old times the people in each village chose from among themselves the people to be in charge of the town. I've even heard said that everyone in the town got together to discuss things. Maybe in places like this. Don't know if it's true. It's forbidden, of course, to read about the history of the Before Time. For our own good, the Rulers say."

Leora turned this over in her mind. "Why do we need Rulers? And guards?"

Howie, out of habit, said, "Shhhhhh," and looked

over his shoulder. "Don't let anyone hear you talking like that. They'll send you . . ." Howie stopped in mid-sentence.

Leora knew what Howie had been about to say, but she pretended not to have noticed.

"So why do we need the Rulers?" Howie repeated the question. "It's like if you're in a boat, you do what the captain says. You don't mutiny. Or jump out into the middle of the sea."

"But we're not in a boat."

"Well, we might as well be. For one, there's the birmbas. Now who's got the guns? Not you or me. The guards have the guns. We need them around to keep us from getting eaten alive."

"But what if the birmbas aren't really bad? What if they're only trying to protect themselves?"

"Wellll . . ."

Leora could tell that Howie was not convinced on the subject of the birmbas.

"And, for another thing," he continued, "there's the problem of the food."

"But the people farm their own food."

"Yes, but who protects them from the birmbas while they do it? And who's in charge of the winter supplies? And who brings in goods from other nations in the south when the winter stuff runs out? We'd starve to death now, wouldn't we?"

Leora was doing her best to ignore the nervousness in the fingers of her webbed hand.

"But, Howie," she said, "if the guards didn't take the food away in the first place, the people could save it themselves. And besides, in the meantime, there's lots of winter food in the woods, like what the birmbas eat. Barka nuts, and nitta berries, and roots that I've eaten —and lots of other new-species, I'm sure."

Their conversation was cut short by a sound at the entry.

"Tomo?" Leora said hopefully to Howie. But the trembling in her left hand told her differently.

In the next second, they heard voices! And heavy boots!

"Shhhhhh," Howie whispered in alarm, dowsing the candle. "It's guards!"

Though they could make out the sound of two voices, at first the words were indistinguishable. For one terrible moment, one voice got louder, closer and clearer. "There's no roof in the next room," it said. "We're better off in here." The voice retreated and they heard a scraping and scuffling as the guards settled in the big entry room.

Leora and Howie froze.

Then Howie whispered, "We're going to have to go out the window of the middle room. We'll make a dash for it. I'll jump first and lift you down."

Leora didn't move. The last time she'd overheard

guards talking, she'd learned a potentially valuable piece of information: that they were planning to infiltrate the rebels' group with a spy.

Who knows? Perhaps this time she could learn even more. If Reba was alive, and if she was a rebel, anything Leora could learn might be of value.

"No, Howie," she whispered. "I'm going to listen. You wait here."

And before he had a chance to stop her, she was creeping into the empty rainy room that separated them from the guards.

By the time Howie caught up with her, she was to the far end of it, planted near the doorway, out of sight, but within easy earshot.

Howie tugged at her sleeve imploringly. But Leora could only think of Reba.

"It's no wonder they call it a ghost town," she heard a young voice say. "This place gives me the creeps."

His statement was answered by an indistinguishable grumble.

"The people say," the first voice continued, "that every time a child disappears in the forest, its ghost walks the woods looking for shelter."

"The people!" the lower voice scoffed. "The people are a pack of sheep. Herd them. But pay them no mind."

"A fellow I know," the younger voice continued unabashed, "a guard, tells how he was on a march some years back. Must have been six or seven years. The summer after that child disappeared from Village Three. Says he saw her ghost."

He paused, and Leora could imagine him looking around nervously, as if he, too, might see it at any minute. When he went on, his voice was more than a little nervous. "One night in the fog, it was. Red hair and all. Saw her one minute, next minute she'd vanished into thin air."

"Hah!" the deeper voice barked. "Some guards are no better than sheepdogs! Listen to the people too much, that's their trouble. Me, I know which side my bread is buttered on. What's the first thing they teach you at the Academy? That the people are like animals. That it's our job to keep them in their pens—their separate pens, mind you—and teach them obedience. Don't you forget it."

The younger man gave a noncommittal mumble.

"Fah!" cursed the deeper voice. "Let's check in the room past the next for something drier. Unless," he added snidely, "you're afraid of ghosts."

Leora, barely able to contain her anger as she listened to their conversation, held her breath. She sensed Howie tensing himself for battle. She knew his hand would be on his knife by now. She also knew that he was no match for two guards with guns. She braced herself.

But at that moment the silence was shattered by a

splintering crash and the landing of something enormous, followed by a scream of terror.

"Birmba!" shouted one of the guards.

"It's Tomo!" Leora whispered to Howie.

"The musket won't fire! The powder's wet!" wailed the younger guard.

"To the back room!" barked the older guard. "We can lock ourselves in!"

Now they'd be caught for sure. Leora thought she heard Howie muttering a prayer.

The impulse came to her in a flash. She let out what she hoped was a ghostlike wail.

"*Eeeeoooo.*"

Encouraged by the gasps on the other side of the door, she threw her hood over her head and drifted forward.

"*Eeeeaaahhhh!*"

She swayed in the doorway, her webbed hand illuminated by a shaft of moonlight.

It was the older of the two guards, the one who didn't believe in ghosts, whose terrified face confronted her.

"Sainted mercy! It's a phantom!"

She gave one final, bloodcurdling wail.

Apparently the sight of a spirit was even more dreadful than the threat of a birmba. The two guards spun around, then, shoving and cursing, they tore past Tomo, out the door, and into the night.

Tomo pursued them briefly, with an occasional roar for good measure.

By the time he reappeared in the doorway, Leora was prancing about with delight, trying to muffle her laughter. Howie was doing a poor job of stifling his hoarse guffaw, and it wasn't long before Tomo, too, succumbed to an attack of something suspiciously like the hiccups.

"G-O-O-D J-O-B," said Howie to Tomo, gesturing as he enunciated each word with care. Then he exploded joyfully, "No one could have done it better, mates! You two sailors routed those pirates like you were the queen's own navy. Which is a very good thing. Because when things are wrong beyond wrong, a man needs to mutiny. And a man who needs to mutiny needs some very good mates indeed!

"Sheep in pens indeed!" he exclaimed. "Well, here's three as won't be sheep anymore.

"And that," he added, "calls for a celebration. And we happen to have some of Norie's finest, salted away. For a rainy day, you might say. Which it is."

Howie rummaged in his pack, pulling out a lumpy bundle. He unwrapped the white dishcloth to reveal a pile of pastries. They were somewhat the worse for wear, but their fruity smell enriched the dank air of the old town hall.

Howie offered one to Leora. She accepted, signaling

with her eyes toward Tomo, knowing it would not occur to Howie otherwise to offer him one.

With a newfound air of respect, Howie made the offer graciously. "Er . . . Tomo. I mean, Mr. Tomo, er . . . mate . . . er . . . sir?"

Tomo hesitated minimally, chose one daintily, and devoured it in a mouthful. Then he graced Howie with a look of such winning gratitude that Howie couldn't but offer him a second.

"Ah!" said Howie, as he watched the second pastry go the way of the first. Then he seized one quickly for himself.

Leora looked at the two of them, Howie and Tomo, side by side, munching companionably. This tea party, she thought, with her own mouth full of sweet berry filling, was more what she had in mind!

Transformation

WHEN LEORA awoke, it was to the impression that the town hall was filled with a noisy throng of people, their voices raised in both disagreement and laughter.

Quickly she realized that what she really heard was the sound of the wind, roaring and whuffling in the great maple that towered over the partially roofless hall. Still, she couldn't entirely banish the sense of presence of the friendly ghosts of her imagination.

Thinking about their night's encounter, she was sorry not to have learned any secrets from the guards. But she was encouraged by the guard's tale of the redheaded *ghost*. Reba must have survived the guards' attack on their father. But where was she now?

If there was news to be found of her anywhere, it would be in Village Fifteen.

From the tilting front steps of Town Hall, Leora surveyed the landscape, no longer shrouded in darkness and rain. Where at one time there had been buildings, there were now odd-shaped mounds—stones overgrown and clothed in moss, like a herd of soft green sheep grazing the hillocks.

A cheeping sound brought her eyes to a busy nest in a lower branch of a maple. A sparrow was filling the eager mouths of three young offspring. As it flew off, Leora watched as one of the young birds wobbled bravely on the edge of the nest. She put her own arms out wide and imagined being ready to fly.

Howie looked up from packing his knapsack and smiled.

"Can you smell it?" he asked.

Leora sniffed. It was something more than pine.

"It's the sea," he said.

Leora knew that Howie had only been to the sea once, as a boy, and that all of his sea talk he'd learned from a very old storybook—one of the forbidden ones that had survived from the Before Time.

"Hauling lobster. That's what I'd be doing," he mused now with pleasure. "Like my great-great-granddaddies.

" 'Cept there's nor lobster nor fish left after the Disaster. Leastwise not ones you can eat. Just new-species, they say. And anyways," he said, shaking himself back to reality, "it's forbidden to go to the sea."

"Why is it forbidden, Howie?"

"I 'spect the real reason is the Rulers have no navy

theirselves. Could be they don't want folks going here and there without the guards to mind them. But what I wouldn't give for a boat of me own!" His eyes were looking far away. And it wasn't at the trees.

She could feel her hand moving, as if already sketching his boat. "You *will* have a boat, Howie," she said.

He chuckled. "Coming from you . . . Well, I'd best be deciding what color to paint her then.

"Yo!" he exclaimed. "Now how'd I forget a thing like that. Lookee here what Norie sent you." He held a tidy packet of drawing paper in one hand and a charcoal stick in the other.

"Oh! Thank you, Norie!" she said, as if Norie were there. "And thank you, Howie," she added, as she claimed her treasure. "I've been collecting pictures in my mind."

Leora stowed the paper and charcoal in her pack.

Howie joined her on the steps. "This will be our last morning on the road," he said. "In a few hours we'll be heading into Village Fifteen."

"That's what I wanted to talk to you about," Leora said. "If the guards learn that I'm alive, they'll still want to send me to the Institute. I'll need to be disguised."

"Ahead of me again, aren't you?" Howie's eyes twinkled.

"If you'll cut my hair," Leora continued, "I'll go into the village as a boy."

Howie squinted at her, then gave a grunt of acquiescence.

"If only I had a needle and thread," she said regretfully, "I could turn my skirt into a pair of pants."

"Well, if a hook and line ain't as good as a mackerel. I've got a needle—a fat one for sewing leather. And some heavy line, too," Howie said, getting into the spirit of things. "Not to mention a pair of shears to boot. We choppers are fit up with most everything."

∵

Shortly, Howie had his shears in hand. "You're sure about this now?"

"Of course. It will grow back," Leora said sensibly.

"Norie'd do a better job of it, that's sure," Howie said, reluctantly closing the shears on a thick sheaf of hair just over her ear.

Leora liked the crunchy sound the shears made as they cut through her hair. As the hair dropped to the ground, she took a deep breath as if she had just been relieved of a weight she had been unaware of carrying.

Howie was quiet as he fine-tuned her haircut. At last he said, "It's not to fret you again that I bring this up." His scissors were still as he spoke. "Most like it won't be a problem. Well, it's just this. What I want to say . . . if we meet any problems up ahead . . . if anything happens to me . . . well, I want you to go right on and find the rebels."

Leora was silent. Howie went on, "If something happens to me . . . well, it won't make no never mind. But you . . . well, that's a different kettle of fish."

Howie paused, then continued. "For one: Someone's got to tell the rebels about the birmbas—about them being friendly and all. It means we don't need the guards like we thought. And for two: Someone's got to tell them 'bout this new-species grub. They could use that—to know that folks could survive a winter, even without the Rulers' winter food supply."

He looked at her now. "So what do you say? I mean, to keeping yourself safe, even if things don't work out for me?"

Leora fingered her locket. She sighed. And at last she nodded. Inside of herself, she knew she was agreeing to do a great deal more than Howie was asking of her.

"Well then, that's settled," he said, business concluded.

He stepped back from her, admiring the final effect. "Not so bad after all."

Leora ran her fingers through her new head of hair. It was curlier than before. She liked the feel of it.

Before long, using Howie's needle and twine, she had turned her skirt into a pair of pants. She thought they looked a little odd, but when she strode back and forth modeling her new outfit, Howie said, "Well, I'll be scuttled!" clearly impressed.

She leaped up onto a large boulder, then down, and over the trunk of a fallen spruce.

"Shipshape!" said Howie, his eyes widening. "Just shipshape!"

Leora wished that she had made the change earlier on in her journey. She enjoyed her new agility. She threw back her shoulders. She felt unencumbered and . . . freer? She thought she might even be stronger, and experimentally hefted her knapsack. Definitely stronger!

When they had wound their way down between the mossy foundations toward the woods below, Tomo joined them. But as they moved along, Leora couldn't help noticing that he was prowling and pacing. He was like an anxious dog with two thoughts in his mind at once. Did Tomo know something they didn't?

But she was enjoying the feeling of her new identity too much to worry. Her new sense of strength brought with it a new confidence: confidence not only that they could find Reba, but that then she, Leora, could be of help to her. She increased the length of her stride, swinging her arms wide.

Approaching the warmer climate of the coast was like walking into spring. Drifts of starflowers, bunchberries, and mayflowers brightened their path. With a new pad of paper in her pack, Leora's fingers itched to be drawing.

She spread her webbed hand wide before her. Regretfully, she realized that she would have to start hiding her hand again. She tucked it experimentally into her cape. She discovered with surprise that it felt different from when she had kept it hidden before. It snuggled cozily now into the safety of her pocket. Like a bird in its nest, she thought.

She was surprised by a rush of warmth in her hand. Suddenly she found herself remembering how she had sat, drawing, by the window in the kitchen pantry, on that day that seemed so long ago. She remembered the appearance beneath her moving charcoal of that pair of eyes among the leaves. Eyes of a birmba. A birmba she had no way of knowing she was about to encounter.

She shrank from the thought.

There were things about her hand she just didn't want to know.

To the Village

IT WAS LATE in the afternoon when she noticed that Tomo's odd behavior had grown odder still. Now he was eyeing Howie in a peculiar way.

That's when it hit her. They would have to leave Tomo behind!

She had grown so accustomed to his company. He was part of her life. Her new life. How could she possibly leave him behind?

"Howie," she said. "Tomo can't come into Village Fifteen."

"I'd like to see the looks on folks' faces if he did! But the guards would put more bullets in him than a porcupine has quills. No, we'll have to leave him. And pretty soon at that."

He looked at her. "You'll miss the critter, won't you?"

Then he looked at Tomo. "I'll be missing him m'self, nows I think on it."

They traveled on in silence. At last Howie stopped.

"Just past this stand of cedars you'll see the village," he said.

They approached the edge of the forest cautiously. Leora peered out through the screen of the cedar leaves.

"There's vegetable gardens between here and the town wall," Howie explained, his voice hushed. "Their Edgeland has no fence around it like ours. So they just use lots of guards to protect the croptenders from the birm—" Howie stopped short in embarrassment. "No offense, mate," he apologized to Tomo.

There were, indeed, lots of guards standing idly among the bent backs of the croptenders. And beyond them lay a village quite unlike her own. The houses seemed to be made of wood, instead of the heavy stone of the houses in Village Three.

"They have young children tending the crops here!" Leora exclaimed.

"That's so. The guards ask more of these folks than in our parts."

"Why?"

"Dunno. They call 'em *foreigners*. And these folks being here a hundred years and more! Their skin is darker, true. And they do talk another language when there's no one abouts. Strictly forbidden, of course, but they do."

Leora remembered Norie's tale of a group of traveling

blueberry pickers, who had believed in Grand Nan's drawing and had helped her prepare for the Disaster. Again she felt that rush of energy in her hand.

"But, Howie, even if they were 'from away' . . . that's no reason to treat them hard. And look. Some of those children working, they can't be more than five years old!"

"Well, it's a lucky thing for us there *are* children there. On account of once we manage to sneak that far, they'll think we're *both* picking crops. And a lucky thing you've grown as brown as a berry out in the sun these days."

"Won't they notice the new faces?"

"The guards don't look much at faces. Any more than they'd notice a new sheep in the pack. You heard 'em. The people are like animals, is what they said." Howie's voice held a note of bitterness that Leora had never heard before.

"Lookee there," he said. "At that clump of highbush cranberry. It'll be an easy scoot from here to there. Then we'll work our way down back along them firs, to the end of that plot of peas—and start picking! There's extra baskets there at the end."

Leora was only half listening. She was thinking about Tomo. Tomo who had found her water when she was thirsty and food when she was hungry. Tomo who had woven night-nests for her. How could she make him understand why she had to leave him?

"Oh, Tomo," she said sadly. She reached out and stroked the rough fur of his forearm with her webbed hand. If thoughts *could* flow through her hand, she hoped it would happen now.

Of course she could not expect him to understand that she had to find her sister. If she had a sister, that is.

"Don't you worry now, mate," Howie said to him. "I'll be keeping watch over her. And next we meet, I'm going to cook us up some nice calpa root porridge. My own recipe. You'll see. Though I 'spect you won't be holding your appetite for that event," he said with a twinkle.

Then he continued, gravely, "So we're off now. And you're not to follow. You understand? S-T-A-Y H-E-R-E." Howie mouthed the words slowly and carefully, as if Tomo might be able to read his lips.

No sooner were these words out of Howie's mouth than Tomo broke away from Leora's touch and placed himself squarely in front of Howie.

"Well, I'll miss you, too, mate, but we've got to leave." Howie tried to sidestep, but Tomo moved, blocking his path again.

"Tomo!" Leora said. "Stop that! You know Howie. He's your friend."

The harder Howie tried to get past Tomo, the more insistent Tomo became.

"Get ready, Leora," Howie said. "I don't know what this is about, but we're a-going to have to make a run for it. The croptenders have begun gathering up to go back for dinner, and if we don't sneak down there with them fast, we'll miss our chance."

"Tomo! Stop!" Leora begged.

"When I count three, Leora," Howie said urgently.

Tomo's body seemed to grow wider and ready for action.

"One. Two. Three. Go!"

As if that were the signal Tomo had been waiting for, he knocked Howie flat on his back, and pinned him there with a great furry foot.

"Stop it, Tomo! Let him go!" Leora's voice rose in exasperation. "That's *bad*! *Shame* on you! Let him go! Now! I order you. Let him go!"

Tomo's eyes met her own. For some moments he didn't move. Then slowly he released Howie, shook himself, and turned his eyes away from hers.

"Leora! Now!" said Howie, leaping to his feet. "This is our last chance. Run!"

Leora caught one final look from Tomo as she followed Howie. "Ohhhhh, Tomo," she moaned as they skirted the flowering highbush cranberries, just beyond the forest edge. "Good-bye, good-bye, good-bye," she whispered. But by then she knew they were too far away for Tomo to hear. She wiped her tears with her sleeve and did her best to keep close to Howie as they dove for the cover of the fir trees.

"Here's our last dash now, Leora! If we can just get

behind that stack of empty baskets, we're home free."

The escort guards, too, must have been hungry for their dinner. Their attention was turned toward the town as the croptenders straggled back toward the village's wide gateway.

Before Leora knew it, she and Howie, with baskets in hand, were plodding after the weary croptenders, trying to look as if they, too, had spent a hard day in the fields. Leora looked hungrily at the pickers' baskets of tender green peas.

As Leora came abreast of a boy somewhat smaller than herself, she peeked out of the corner of her eye at his brown skin, his glossy black hair. He glanced sideways at her. His eyes widened in surprise and he almost stopped in his tracks. For a moment she was afraid that he would alert the guard. Instead, he gave a discreet nod, as if to say, "all's safe."

As they neared the village gateway, its heavy doors swung open. She looked at the pair of red-coated sentries standing woodenly on one side. As she watched, one of them came to life, nudged the other, muttered something and pointed into the crowd of croptenders. Leora's heart stood still. They were pointing at Howie!

"Ho! You! There! Chopper! Halt!"

Howie cursed under his breath and stopped.

"Don't you stop, Leora!" came Howie's gruff whisper. "Go! Find Reba!" His hushed voice was urgent. "Don't fret about me. I'll spin 'em a yarn. Go!"

By now, four of the escort guards had waded through the croptenders and gathered around Howie, lifting him as they bore him away. The croptenders averted their eyes, as if accustomed to such trouble. The village doors swung closed behind them with a thud.

Leora was inside the walls of Village Fifteen. Alone.

In the Village

LEORA PULLED her cape around her and thrust her webbed hand deeper into her pocket.

Everything was new to her here. The streets were of dirt, the houses of wood. Even the people looked different. But something about the look in their dark eyes and brown faces made her feel like less of an outcast here than she had felt in Village Three.

Her hand clenched as she became aware of a guard, less than twenty paces away, facing in her direction. Was he looking at her? Her feet refused to move.

A touch at her left elbow startled her.

"Walk," came the hushed message, "or they'll notice you."

It was the boy from the field.

"You can come home with me," the boy's low voice continued.

Could she trust him? The presence of the guards gave her little choice. Besides, she noticed, her fingers had unclenched in her pocket. At least her *hand* felt safe.

She kept her eyes on the ground in front of her, only darting an occasional glance at her companion. He wore a cape of rough undyed wool: a blanket that hung in front and in back, with a hole for his head in the middle.

So these, she thought, were the people who had believed in Grand Nan's drawing, who had worked with her to prepare for the Disaster.

"My name is Yano," the boy said, speaking out loud now as they rounded a bend into a narrow alleyway. "That's short for Emiliano." His voice rose and fell in a pleasant manner. "It is a name from our language. A language called Spanish."

"I'm Leo—" Leora remembered her male identity in the nick of time. "My name is Leon," she concluded.

"Leon," Yano repeated. He eyed her assessingly, then nodded.

He must know, she thought, that it was her friend whom the guards had taken. What will they do with him? she wanted to ask. But she knew that in asking it, she might be inviting questions she was unwilling to answer.

The street had grown narrower and the houses smaller and closer together. They stopped at a ramshackle building the color of pale egg yolk. It was made of a series of small connected structures and had been decorated with playful curlicues of wooden trim.

Yano went in ahead of her.

"Enter," he said, bowing slightly.

She paused. Once inside, it would be hard to leave. But where else could she go?

"Please," Yano said, inviting her in for the second time.

Accepting his invitation, she found herself in a dim, low-ceilinged room. Its walls were lined with fat spools of yarn in a rainbow of colors. In the far corner stood a large rough wooden loom, stretched with a half-finished woolen blanket, not unlike the one that Yano wore.

The rich, steamy smell of food reminded Leora that she was hungry.

"*Mamá!*" Yano called.

The woman who peeked her round face into the room was not much taller than Leora. The eyes in the dark face revealed a mixture of surprise and concern. In her hand was a loaf of dark brown bread.

"Yano?" she said.

Yano launched into a rapid flow of Spanish. While his mother glanced repeatedly at Leora, a girl of three or four peered out from behind her mother, invisible but for a single alarmed eye and a tiny hand that clutched the woman's apron.

When Yano's mother finally answered him, Leora distinguished the word *papá*.

"One moment, please," Yano said to Leora, moving toward the back of the house. "My father is also home from work. I will be right back."

Yano's mother was left nodding and smiling at Leora, while the child behind her tried desperately to tug her out of the doorway and back into the safety of the kitchen.

"Margarita is very shy," Yano's mother said. "Please don't be offended. She has always been like this. She trusts only us." The little girl murmured fearfully and tugged harder than ever on the apron.

Soon Yano reappeared with a man not much taller than his mother. His cape, similar to Yano's, bore bits of wood shavings. His eyes, set wide in a broad face, took Leora in but gave away nothing.

Had she done the right thing? She felt sure that Yano wished her well. But would his parents feel it safe to harbor her, putting their family in danger? Maybe they would ask her to leave. Or worse, turn her over to the guards. Should she just open the door and run?

As much as anything else, it was the face of Yano's little sister that anchored her. There was something about the quality of the young girl's fear that reminded Leora of Wiggala—Wiggala when she had first discovered him in the cage in the basement. It had been her webbed hand, she reminded herself, that had won him over.

Leora hesitated. She crouched down and took a cautious duck step toward the child, warily extending her left hand, her fingers together so that the webbing would be invisible. She stroked the hard knuckles of the girl's tiny hand and felt it grow calm.

"No, Leon!" Yano gasped. "She will have a terrible fit!"

But Leora wasn't paying attention to Yano. Nor was Margarita. The little hand on the apron unclenched. The frightened whimpering stopped, and not one but two eyes now appeared from behind the voluminous skirt.

As Yano and his parents watched in astonishment, Margarita threw Leora a timid grin and began to take advantage of her position behind her mother to strike up a game of peekaboo.

"*Mire no más!*" Yano's mother exclaimed.

"So," said Yano's father at last. "It appears that Margarita has decided it. If even *she* will trust you, well, we must trust you, too." Yano grinned.

"Pass, please," Yano's mother said warmly, inviting her into the kitchen. "*Está su casa.*"

"That," said Yano, as Leora entered the warmth of the sweet-smelling kitchen, "means, 'This is your house.' "

In the Yellow House

"MY PARENTS, Mr. and Mrs. del Valle," said Yano, conducting the introductions formally. "Leon."

"So your name is León," Mr. del Valle said, pronouncing it with an accent on the last syllable.

Leora looked down at the clay-tiled floor and mumbled assent, feeling uncomfortably that this was the moment at which she might be expected to explain herself.

"In the language of my ancestors," said Mr. del Valle, asking no questions, "that means *lion*. You are small for a lion. But perhaps," he went on generously, "you are courageous like a lion."

Yano's mother added something quickly in Spanish.

The man nodded. "My wife says perhaps you are hungry like a lion, too."

Leora flushed, realizing she had been staring at the loaf of bread in the woman's hand.

As Yano cleared the table, and Mrs. del Valle worked at the stove, Leora studied the kitchen. Its walls were covered with small weavings and brightly painted wooden carvings. Rough shelves held rows of clay pots and dishes, glazed and decorated with fanciful patterns. Although it was very different from Norie's kitchen, it had the same feeling of hominess. And the same sense of . . . safety.

Margarita summoned her with a tug back toward the living room. There, Leora found the contents of her knapsack spread out on the floor. The little girl squatted and lovingly stroked the surface of a piece of textured ivory paper. Leora knelt on the floor beside her.

She wished that she could draw with her right hand. But in the low light, if she was careful to keep the fingers of her webbed hand together, her secret would be safe enough.

She paused before she set her charcoal to the paper.

It was the paper that Howie had given her in Town Hall. Before he had been taken by the guards. Before they had to leave Tomo. She was half afraid that her hand, with a mind of its own, would draw a picture of her two friends, eating pastry together.

Or, worse still, that it would draw a picture of . . . she felt an alarming rush of energy in her fingertips . . . a picture of . . . *something that had not yet happened.*

Margarita nudged her impatiently.

Well, this wasn't the time or the place for that kind of drawing. If it was in her power to do so, she would prevent her hand from doing anything out of the ordinary. She concentrated hard and set charcoal to paper.

To her enormous relief, what emerged in the curling lines beneath her charcoal was a likeness of Margarita herself. In the picture, the little girl was seated at the kitchen table. Her face bore a look of surprise and delight as she cocked her head to look at the jaunty bird that perched on her shoulder.

While Margarita, beside her, uttered mysterious little exclamations of delight, Leora added a few whimsical details to the background. When it was done, she examined the drawing. Although the energy in her hand still surged like an underground stream, she had drawn nothing disturbing.

If she were to draw a second picture, she might not be so lucky.

Fortunately, Margarita was satisfied with the first. Tugging Leora back into the kitchen, she presented it to her brother with a torrent of Spanish.

Yano grinned and said something to his sister. Margarita looked at Leora in surprise.

"I told her you are a boy," Yano said, laughing, to Leora. "All this time she thought you were a girl!"

His face grew serious as he turned his eyes to the drawing.

"You can draw, Leon!" he said in wonder. "*Mire, Mamá.*"

Mrs. del Valle lit the candles, and held the picture under the light. She nodded. "Like real," she said. "Exactly like real."

"You draw like an angel, León," Mr. del Valle said, examining the picture. "In our village there is great respect for the gift of drawing."

Again, the energy in her hand surged.

"But that is a long story," he added, pulling a chair out invitingly for her. "A story for another time. Now," he said, winking at Leora, "it is time to feed our hungry lion."

Margarita scrambled into a chair beside her. She bowed her head, showing off a pair of delicately crafted brass barrettes that held back her sleek black hair. Leora was reminded of Wiggala and his love of shiny things.

"Very nice," said Leora, admiring the proud possessions.

"Soup of peas," said Mrs. del Valle as she ladled a thick green soup into bowls all around.

Nothing had looked so inviting to Leora in a long time, or tasted so good. The soup made her think of the calpa root porridge that Howie had promised to make for Tomo. How she wished Howie were here to eat the soup with her! Again she saw Howie being borne away by the guards. Again she saw the look on Tomo's face as she yelled at him.

Maybe she could talk to the del Valles. About everything. She felt so comfortable with them that the questions that hovered on the tip of her tongue seemed ready to pop out of her of their own accord.

Like, *What do the guards do to men when they take them prisoner?*

And, *What do you know about the rebels?*

And most of all, *Is there anyone in the village with red hair?*

If she didn't ask about Reba, how would she ever find her?

But . . . if she asked the wrong people at the wrong time—she didn't even want to think about it.

"Tasa," Margarita was saying, thrusting her little earthenware cup in front of Leora. "*ES-TA ES U-NA TA-SA.*"

A language lesson. Leora smiled. There was something familiar about her little teacher's manner. What was it?

"Soon it is Margarita who must learn to speak English," Yano said. "She must learn before she's old enough to go to school," he added sadly.

"But when do you go to school if you have to work every day in the fields?" Leora asked.

"We go for one year. Long enough to learn the Forbiddens."

"And to learn to read?"

"To read?" Yano said in surprise. "No. Not to read.

Did children in your village . . ." He stopped himself, apparently reluctant to press her with questions.

"Well, anyway," Yano went on, his voice growing tight. "The teachers are . . ." He rubbed the back of his hand, and Leora noticed a series of scars stretching across his knuckles. ". . . they are not kind," he concluded, with a worried look at his little sister.

For a moment Leora was back in her old schoolroom, singled out for rebuke, cringing under the dislike in Teacher's eyes. Just remembering it, her hand wanted to dive deeper into her cape. But the thought of all the children in Village Fifteen being treated that way . . . or worse . . .

Her right hand went into a fist, and before she knew it, she had brought it down on the table so hard that the bowls rattled. "But that's not fair!"

Margarita's eyes widened.

"Fair?" Yano looked at her.

"No! It's not fair!" In her mind she could hear Howie saying, When things are wrong beyond wrong, a man needs to mutiny.

"León, things have not been fair for our people for so long," said Mr. del Valle, sounding a little bit like Norie when she was gathering energy for a story. "When our people came to this country in the Before Time, they wandered about like a flock of homeless birds, picking the fruit crops wherever they were ripe, and, well . . .

they were not made very welcome. But we will always remember that once, just before the Disaster . . ." Mr. del Valle looked as if he were remembering. ". . . well, someone made us at home."

For a second, Leora felt as if Grand Nan were sitting there with them at the table. Beneath her cape, her hand flitted like a caged bird that had something to do, somewhere to go.

The rest of the talk that night wove easily back and forth between English and Spanish. Margarita insisted that Leora be told stories from very very long ago. From a time in the distant past when the villagers' ancestors had ruled their own distant land. And how these proud ancestors had been conquered by cruel people from across the sea and made slaves in their own country.

Leora noticed that when the del Valles talked about the Before Time, they did not lower their voices, or look over their shoulders, as Norie did when she spoke of things forbidden-to-tell. As if they spoke about such things often. It was almost as if they lived on the other side of some invisible line.

All the while, the del Valles' warm glances included her, embraced her, lulled her. Was this what it felt like to have a family? In the warm light of the candles, Leora found herself growing so sleepy that she half imagined that Reba was sitting there at the table, too, her red hair glowing in the yellow light.

"*ES-TA ES U-NA TA-SA.*" Margarita, continuing with her language lesson, eyed her expectantly.

That was it! That was the way Howie had talked to Tomo at first, one syllable at a time. Leora started to giggle sleepily at this thought. But suddenly she wasn't laughing anymore. She was crying. Right there at the dinner table. In front of people she hadn't even known for a day!

Leora wanted so badly to tell them everything.

I yelled at Tomo, she wanted to say. He knew Howie would be taken and tried to save him. And I yelled at him!

"Enough, Margarita," Mrs. del Valle said. "León is tired. It is time for sleep."

Helping Leora out of her chair, she scooped up Margarita and bustled the two of them off into a tiny room behind the kitchen.

"Come. Let me show you to bed. Yano. Bring the blanket from the living room. You will sleep here, León, with Margarita and Yano." Mrs. del Valle indicated an inviting feather comforter on the floor almost as big as the room itself.

I'm afraid the guards might kill Howie, Leora wanted to tell her. Mrs. del Valle settled Margarita in the corner with a kiss, and, using the blanket which Yano had produced, tucked the two of them in.

I am looking for my sister! Leora wanted to shout. And I don't even know if she is dead or alive!

"Sleep well, children," said Mrs. del Valle, leaving the darkened room. "And do not be worried, León. For as long as you need, this is your house."

"*Está su casa*, León," Margarita muttered sleepily under the blankets.

Leora listened to the soft breathing beside her, and to the rhythmic click clack of the great wooden loom.

She wondered how much longer she would be able to keep it all inside herself. Not just the worries and the questions but the surging energy in her hand, which, like the gathering force of a great wave, she feared would soon be too powerful to contain.

Meeting in the Night

LEORA AWOKE suddenly. She sat bolt upright in bed, as wide awake and clear as if she had not been sleeping at all. Yano and Margarita slept soundly next to her. She was briefly aware of the soft voices of the del Valles in the kitchen.

She felt as if she had been called awake to a purpose. Had the del Valles called her? She thought not.

Then it began. First her hand began to itch as it did when she thought about drawing. Then came the surging of energy that had been troubling her during the day. It gathered force and was soon accompanied by an even more disturbing phenomenon. It was as if she hovered at the edge of a dream—a dream that threatened to break through and become real at any moment.

She reached for her knapsack by the bed and took out her paper and charcoal. In the dim light, she had a fleeting impression that a picture was already there, the ghost of an image floating on top of the ivory pad. Then it was gone.

But as the force in her hand took over, an image swelled up from the darkness within her. Her charcoal flew back and forth over the paper with the speed of a bird in flight. The image crested and flowed with a rush onto the paper.

Gradually, like a sleeper just awakened, she surfaced. She studied the picture in front of her with curiosity, as if it had been drawn by someone else.

She recognized the buildings. They were the buildings at the entry gate of Village Fifteen, flanked by apple trees heavy with fruit. And there were guards. Guards brandishing long sticks, which seemed to be burning. She noticed with horror that one of the buildings was burning—the guards were setting fire to it! Were they trying to burn the whole village?

Leora had no doubt that the picture she had drawn told the truth. When or why it would come to pass, she didn't know. But she knew that it would.

She was glad that she could still hear the hushed voices of Mr. and Mrs. del Valle in the kitchen, that she wouldn't have to wait till morning to warn them. Moving with care so as not to wake her bedmates, she crept toward the kitchen door.

There was a noticeable tension in the hushed conversation. To her surprise, it was in English. And she could clearly distinguish an unfamiliar male voice.

She stopped in her tracks.

"I've a message for you from the rebels," the visitor was saying. "They've asked me to start spreading the word among my tribe. But it is not my own village I worry about. The Rulers will not be expecting trouble there. The guards think my people haven't the brains of the cows in the fields. Their ignorance is our protection.

"But here," he continued somberly, "it is a different story."

"What news do you have, Lex, about Village Fifteen?" Mrs. del Valle asked.

"It's just a rumor, of course," he answered. "And you never know who to trust. But the word is that the guards are collecting a list of suspected rebel sympathizers. And that one of these days they'll sweep through the village and take them all. You must be careful, my friends."

"No, it is you who must be careful, Lex," Mr. del Valle said with concern. "Us, we know nothing of importance. But you, you know where the rebels are hidden, and you know some of the rebels by sight and by name. If the guards suspect you, they will have cruel ways of getting that information from you."

"Well, for our own protection, no single one of us knows everything. Even if they could make me talk, my information is limited."

A board creaked beneath Leora's foot.

Immediately, the visitor was upon her, pulling her swiftly from the shadows into the kitchen.

The del Valles stared at Leora.

"We didn't know you were awake, León," Mr. del Valle said. Leora knew what he meant was *we didn't know you were listening.*

Unafraid, she studied the man beside her. His black hair was drawn back in a braid, emphasizing his broad features. His skin was dark as old leather and deeply creased. It was an interesting face. Instinctively she trusted him. Her hand trusted him.

"I need to know where they are," she said as simply as if she had been a member of the conversation all along.

"Who is this boy?" the visitor asked after a stunned silence. "How long has he been listening?"

"You need to know where *who* is, León?" Mr. del Valle said at last.

"The rebels," she said.

"So have they stooped to using children as spies?" said the man called Lex. His face was impassive, but his voice was a mix of controlled rage and despair. "How did he trick you into taking him in?"

The figures at the table were frozen in the flickering light of the candle.

Leora's heart sank as she understood the implications of the man's statement and the look on the del Valles' faces. *They* were on the side of the rebels. But they thought *she* was a spy. A spy who had just overheard too much. Much too much. For a minute she wondered if this was just a bad dream, or if she and the others were merely figures in one of her drawings.

"I am not a spy!" she said, suddenly outraged at the very suggestion of it. The fervor in her voice brought a look of hope back to the faces of the del Valles. But there was no change in the expression on the face of their guest.

"And now?" he said to the del Valles as if she hadn't even spoken. His voice was grim. "What shall we do with him?"

The ominous tone in his voice brought Mrs. del Valle to her feet. She put her arm protectively around Leora, making every effort to hustle her out of the kitchen and back into the safety of the bedroom. "You are wrong, Lex. He is just a child. Of course he is not a spy. He is a good boy. You will not harm him. Come. Back to bed with you, León. It is cold in here."

But Leora would not allow herself to be budged.

"I am not a spy. I am looking for my sister. If she is alive, she is with the rebels. And someone has to stop this village from being burned."

The last sentence caught Lex's attention.

"Burned?"

She put the drawing on the table.

"Look," she said. "The picture only shows the fire just beginning. Maybe it could be stopped before the whole village burns." She thought about Margarita and Yano. "It has to be stopped!"

"Look," said Mrs. del Valle, pointing at the burning building. "It is the food storage building."

"Who drew this?" Lex demanded.

"I did," Leora answered, her statement supported by nods of agreement from the del Valles.

"He can draw," Mr. del Valle assured their guest. "Some very pretty pictures."

"But this is not a pretty picture. It is a different kind of drawing," Leora said, urgently. "It came by itself. This drawing is the future." As she spoke the words, all doubt evaporated.

"It is a gift," she said, "from Grand Nan."

"Your grandmother, León?" said Mrs. del Valle.

Leora hesitated. She could almost feel the presence of Grand Nan there in the tiny kitchen. It made her feel strong and not afraid.

"My mother's mother's mother's mother," she said. "She drew a picture, too. Long ago. Of the Disaster. Before it even happened." Leora paused to remember the story. "At first," she began, "nobody believed it. But then . . ."

"Santa Maria!" Mrs. del Valle said in awe.

"I think we know the story, León," Mr. del Valle said as he stared at Leora.

At last he nodded. "Our ancestors were good friends of this Grand Nan of yours. The people in our village owe their existence to her. And to her sight. You are welcome in our house twice over, León."

But Lex looked far from convinced.

"It was one of my people in Village Two," he said, "who made something special for the lady you mention. Many winters past." Leora knew he was challenging her to tell him exactly what the "special" thing might be.

She hesitated, then drew out her locket from beneath her collar.

The del Valles and Lex stood transfixed by the half-moon of silver that dangled from her fingertips.

"But it was for her daughter's daughter's daughter's *daughter*," said Lex. "You are a *boy*."

Leora could feel herself blushing.

"Ahhhhh," said Mr. del Valle victoriously. "Yano *told* us he thought León was not your true name."

"And Margarita was right," added Mrs. del Valle with delight. "Margarita thought you were a girl from the first." Mrs. del Valle was obviously pleased by her guest's new identity.

Leora answered the question in their eyes. "My name is Leora."

The del Valles' visitor looked at her gravely. His eyes grew distant, as if he had retreated to some inner world. Then he got to his feet.

"And I am Lex." He addressed Leora solemnly, with a tone of deepest respect. "In my own language, my full name means Soaring Bird. I am of the tribe of the People of the First Light.

"I hope you will forgive my behavior," he continued. "Sometimes the truth hides in the silence. When I am too sure that I know things, I forget to listen to that silence.

"It is not a small gift, Leora: to be able to see the way in which all-that-is-so is woven together. Perhaps," he said thoughtfully, "your gift is even greater than your great-great-grandmother's. In time, you will know."

Leora looked at the drawing on the table, and this time she saw beyond it. Her fingers spread, and for a minute her hand felt as powerful as the wing of a giant bird in flight.

To the Sea

"A GIRL!" said Yano the next morning, aghast.

"A daughter," said Mrs. del Valle, pleased.

"A lion," said Mr. del Valle, satisfied.

"A sister," said Margarita, in English.

"*ESTA ES UNA TASA,*" said Leora. It was all the Spanish she knew. But it made Yano laugh so much that he appeared to have all but forgiven her for being a girl.

"This is a teacup." Lex translated Margarita's Spanish lesson, adding, "and I am a teapot," just to join in the fun.

The night before, Lex had assured her that the villagers would begin an around-the-clock vigil near the town gates. If the guards couldn't be prevented from burning the village, at least the villagers could be warned in time to escape. He suggested that the event in the picture would occur some months in the future, since the apple trees in the drawing already had fruit.

She understood, then, more clearly than ever, the importance of the next phase of her journey. She would have to leave her newfound family of friends, and without delay!

"The rebels' encampment is on an island," Lex explained. "They are all girls and young women." He added, "I am sorry that I do not know if your sister is among them, Leora. As I said, I have only met a few of them. There is plenty of reason to hope."

"Why are there no men?" Leora asked.

"Men and boys are working under the eyes of the guards every day," said Lex. "They would be missed. But the girls, if they leave, the guards don't notice. And the young ones, they have no children yet to keep them home.

"They will welcome you," Lex went on. "Let me explain how to find them."

～

Leora wished breakfast would last longer. She dreaded saying farewell to her new family. But it was time for Yano to head for work in the fields, and if Leora intended to get outside of the village gates, it would be best to go along with him, disguised as a croptender.

"To keep my new daughter warm," said Mrs. del Valle as she placed a soft, cream-colored poncho over her head, adjusting it over her dark cape.

"Oh, thank you!" Leora buried her nose in it, enjoying the smell of new wool.

"Now they will not be able to tell our little lion from one of us," said Mr. del Valle.

Leora felt Margarita's little fingers slipping something cold into the palm of her hand.

"For me?" said Leora, admiring the ornate curlicues of a delicate hair clip. She could see that Margarita's hair was now pulled back by a single clip. "It's the most beautiful present I've ever been given."

Margarita's sad eyes brightened.

"I have nothing to give you," said Yano sadly.

"But you saved me from the guards!" said Leora.

Yano nodded and stood a little taller.

"How do you say *thank you* in Spanish?" Leora asked.

"*Gracias*," Margarita instructed eagerly.

"*Gracias*," said Leora, looking around at their kind faces. Determined not to cry, she decided not to ask how to say *good-bye*.

As she did her best to smile, Lex held her hand in his. "When the hermit thrush sings, Leora," he said.

She knew that for Lex that meant *soon*. Not *never*.

Once in the street, they joined a stream of other villagers on their way to work in the fields. Because she was safe in her new poncho, no one gave her a second look. But as they approached the gates, Leora was dismayed to see a congregation of red-coated guardsmen.

Yano hastened to reassure her. "It's nothing. They're

on their way to some other village. See? They have two choppers with them."

So they did.

And one of them was Howie!

Was he free, or was he a prisoner?

She searched Howie's face for an answer to this question. Clearly he did not expect to see her clothed in a poncho. Then, she could tell, he recognized her. For a moment she was afraid that he would call out her name and betray them. But he grinned instead and then turned his attention to winding a circlet of cord, whistling unconcernedly.

As she and Yano got closer, he broke into a low-pitched sea shanty.

> Well, I'm to the land, and you're to the sea,
> I long to go with you, my laddie,
> But there's yarn to be spun,
> And weaving to be done,
> And there's none do it better than me,
> No, there's none do it better than me.

Howie's fellow chopper stifled a snort of laughter at hearing Howie sing the woman's lines of the sea shanty. The red-coated officers scowled but were apparently too busy to bother with a rebuke.

Leora knew that the song had been intended to reassure her that he had been able to "spin the guards a yarn" about his presence in Village Fifteen. What Howie didn't know was that she was indeed "to the sea." Wouldn't he have loved to come along!

She edged herself as close as she could to him, and, by way of response, she softly sang the last verse of the song.

> You're home to the land,
> While I'm to the sea,
> I long to stay with you, my bonnie.
> But there's wars to be won,
> Under cannon and gun,
> And there's none do it better than me,
> No, there's none do it better than me.

Howie beamed at her rendition and the mock bravado with which she had sung the final line. She could see that he was eyeing Yano, trying to figure out the connection between them. Yano in turn was sizing up Howie.

"Move along. Move along now!" bellowed one of the guards, eager to get the croptenders out of the way.

The turreted food storage building cast a cold shadow over her as she moved past it. She shuddered.

Then with a last glance at Howie, she crowded out the gate with the others. It was not easy to leave him. Nor would it be easy to leave Yano. But there was no time to waste.

As soon as they got to the fields, when the escorts' backs were turned, she signaled a good-bye to Yano. He responded with a lopsided grin. Then she began working her way back to the forest's edge, in much the way she and Howie had arrived the day before — up past the row of young firs, behind the highbush cranberry, then a dive to the safety of the great cedars. The old trees welcomed her into their protective darkness.

The trees soon thinned, and she found herself heading over open land into the light of the rising sun. Here, the low blueberry bush dominated, mixed in with fragrant sweet fern, laurel, and rhodora. Passage through the scrubby brush was made even easier by the vast areas of granite ledge, as easily traversed as cobblestone.

Lex's directions had been somewhat sketchy, and he had been concerned about her ability to find the way. But Leora was confident that her hand would guide her, as it had before. What she needed to do was to find the point on the coast at which the rebels landed and embarked — a spot Lex had described in detail — and hope to connect with them there.

It was precisely because the area was devoid of trees, and even of large bushes, that the rebels had chosen it as a safe route to their encampment.

"The birmbas," Lex had explained, "will never enter the open land. They only feel safe when they can travel under cover. So the rebels can travel without fear of attack or need for protection."

Leora's heart had fallen when she heard this. Without admitting it to herself, she had been hoping that once out of the village she would find Tomo. But having experienced his preference for deep cover even in the woods, it was obvious to her that this open territory would discourage him. She felt quite exposed herself. If there had been guards around, they could have easily spotted her. But again, Lex had reassured her. The guards, like the birmbas, never traveled here.

"Between Village Fifteen and the ocean," he had explained, "there's nothing. Since people are not allowed to be by the sea, there is no one for the guards to order about. It is just emptiness there. So as long as you can find your way, you will be safe."

Leora had decided not to say anything yet about the birmbas. If it was true that the guards had ways of getting information from people, the less information her new friends had, the safer they would be.

A rosy-breasted mourning dove landed with a noisy fluttering of wings in her path.

"Woooaaooo," it lamented.

Something in its doleful call brought back the dream she had had in the forest. The dream of Wilfert, beckoning to Reba. She pulled her hand out from under her poncho now and held it up to the sun that was breaking through the early-morning mist. She no longer had any doubt that, in one way or another, her dream would come to pass. Would she be able to reach Reba in time to warn her? She quickened her pace, grateful that her hand seemed to guide her surely and steadily. If she was something less than confident about the direction, her hand was not.

By midday the sun shone in a vivid blue sky, and the granite outcroppings were warm to the touch. She carried her new poncho over her shoulder now. As she walked, she ate the lunch that Mrs. del Valle had packed for her—three dense bundles tightly wrapped in what appeared to be corn husks. A little like leftover corn meal mush, with a pleasant but unfamiliar aroma. They were so delicious that she couldn't help eating them all. Except for the crumbs she offered to the dove. Surely she would find some barka trees between here and the sea to take care of her dinner.

Now the mourning dove's plaintive call was replaced by unfamiliar piercing cries far overhead. Could these be the seagulls, which Howie had often told her about? If so, it would confirm her being near to the coast. The wind now shifted and brought with it another confirmation—that unusual smell that Howie had identified for her—was it only yesterday?—as the smell of the sea.

The scent was carried at first in the finest of fogs, a fog that softened the contours of the distant landscape. The blue of the sky began to give way to a luminous white. And now the fog grew denser and floated in wisps over the ground, briefly obscuring everything in its path. Leora was surprised, when it cleared for a moment, to find that the barrens had given way to forest.

Except for the occasional white trunk of a birch, the trees here were evergreens. The firs were putting out their spring growth, little fingers of light green, soft and smooth as cat paws. There were also spruce, and scrubby pine, and some others with which she was unfamiliar. She was disappointed not to see any barka trees. She had been counting on them for her next meal.

As she walked she became aware of a new sound. At first it was no more than a whisper, but the farther she went, the louder it became. It was all around her, like a storm.

Suddenly she emerged into a world of light, sound, and vastness. It was the sea!

Standing at the edge of a steep cliff, she saw a breathtaking spread of rock, water, islands, and sky. She looked down into the roiling water as it surged frothy and fierce into the rock-faced inlet. She was startled by a thunderous belch and moan as the water sucked in and out of an invisible cave below.

"The Dragon's Tongue," Lex had said, "is a sharp projection of rock dividing a deep rocky inlet into two. You'll know why they call it a *dragon's* tongue when you hear it at low tide."

Just then the fog parted, revealing an island not far off the shore. A mere sliver of blue-gray, it floated like a mirage in a seamless blend of silver sea and sky.

The rebels' island!

Now all she needed to do was follow the coastal edge northward to arrive at the actual docking spot. Lex had said that if the rebels were going to be traveling between island and shore, it would not be till late at night, when the tide would be high and the moon near full. Already the hazy glow of the sun was low on the horizon.

As she worked her way up the coast, she found herself on a series of promontories—some of pink rock, some of black, some lending anchor to wind-twisted spruce.

From each new vantage point she marveled at the startling beauty. Her fingers, as if they held a pen, were moving by themselves.

Now she hardly needed her hand to guide her, for here was a well-worn path, a root-covered trail winding downward beneath twisted branches of scrubby pine. At the base of the path she found herself on a low rock shelf.

As if it had been waiting for her, a seagull stood, beak to the wind, perched patiently on a craggy table of stone.

She was glad for the company. The wild expanse of

sea, so exciting at first, made her feel small and lonely in the dimming light.

"I've nothing to feed you," she told the gull regretfully. "And I'm hungry enough to eat pebbles." She longed for some barka nuts. Seeing none, she ventured into the underbrush in a vain search for calpa root. She was rewarded by a discovery of a different sort.

There, hidden amid the trees and brush, was a small green boat.

So the rebels must already be on land! They might even have been in the village at the same time as she. They could be here—as soon as tonight perhaps—on their return to the island.

She knew exhaustion would make it difficult to stay awake till they arrived. She found herself a spot on the shelf of rock where she could lean against a boulder, her poncho rolled behind her head. It wasn't even dark yet, and already it was hard to keep her eyes open.

In her imagination it was Reba herself she would meet here at the landing.

As she struggled to stay awake, she tried to imagine how Reba would look now. But all she could envision was the wild red-haired sister of eleven who had disappeared so long ago.

~

She dreamed that a shadowy form came out of the night. It was Tomo. In her dream, she was sleeping and unable to awaken herself to tell him she was sorry.

Again and again she tried to get the words out of her mouth, but even her tongue had gone to sleep. She dreamed that he was looking in her cape pocket. She tried to tell him that she had no more of Norie's tarts left but that one day she would get him some. But still she slept.

Briefly she awoke, just enough to become aware of the coldness of the stone, the darkness of the night, the lapping of the sea. She must stay awake. But sleep tugged her down again into its lair.

Now she dreamed she was a seagull, perched on a boulder. From her perch, she watched two figures standing over the curled figure of a boy on the rock, conferring quietly.

"No. He's not dead," said one. It was a young woman's voice, soft and low. "But he won't last long if we leave him here. If he doesn't die of exposure, he'll be washed out by the tide."

"Nell! We can't bring him with us." This other voice was higher-pitched, the words more clipped. "It isn't safe! For all you know he's a spy!"

"They wouldn't use a child. And how would they know to leave him here?"

"Perhaps they know our whereabouts. And if it wasn't planned, why is he here, in this very spot? Of the whole coast, how could he have chosen our landing? Even a fox tracking its dinner couldn't have discovered this spot. It is on the way to nowhere. Except to us."

In her dream, she fluttered down from her perch, planted herself by the sleeping figure, and watched the two figures retreat.

Leora came briefly to consciousness. How real her dreams were tonight! She half expected to find the people of her dream beside her. But only the sea murmured. A gust of wind brought the smell of the salt. And again she was tugged into sleep as deep as the ocean.

She dreamed that she was a three-year-old child, sound asleep on the living room floor. She was being wrapped in the scratchy warmth of a wool blanket, then lifted and carried, secure and snug, to her bed.

The child in the dream had no idea who it was that might be carrying her.

She only knew that she was safe.

Island

LEORA ROSE out of sleep on a delicious wave of well-being. This, she thought, is how it used to feel. When she still had a family. Waking in the warmth of her bed. Lingering lazily in her dreams. With pleasure, she remembered one of her dreams—the dream of being carried to her bed.

Bed? Her eyes popped open. She *was* in a bed: tucked securely into a blanket-wrapped mat just the right size. Where was she? And how had she come here?

She must still be asleep. All night her dreams had been so lifelike. She eyed the deep brown wool of her cover. She fingered its rough weft. Could a dream be so real? In the air was the unmistakable smell of food. The smell of frying potatoes. Could a dream be *that* real?

The smell of potatoes made her hope this was not a dream. She sat up slowly and looked around. The mat on which she had been sleeping was one of many in a spacious round room. The room's low walls were formed of upright logs, with an occasional space between them providing light. At the center of the room was a crude woodstove. On one wall hung a huge blanket of rough wool, dyed in soft tones of brown and rust and olive green.

A doorway led into a dark passageway. To where? Did she hear voices? Perhaps it was only the roar of the wind.

But there was no mistaking that wonderful smell.

She slid out from under the warmth of her covers. Her poncho had been placed over her as a blanket. She put on her cape and her shoes, which she found placed neatly beside her pack nearby. Then she threaded her way between the mats toward the inviting smell of food. The dark hall ended in a bright patch of blue cloth, the light glowing through it from the other side.

Yes. There were certainly voices. Many voices, and a chorus of conversations. Leora hesitated at the threshold of the passageway. Should she enter?

It was a mixture of curiosity and hunger that drew her toward the blue curtain. She tried to make sense out of the beehive hum of conversation. She could pick out nothing, except for the name *Nell*.

Nell! She had dreamed of someone named Nell! In that dream, she remembered, she herself had been a seagull. And the young woman Nell had not wanted to abandon the sleeping boy on the rock.

So it had not been a dream! Had the rebels found her and brought her to their hideaway? Was Reba in the next room?

She hesitated. For a moment she was back in the tree nest, Wiggala planted firmly on her chest. She could hear the voice of the guards beneath her: ". . . let her recruit one of our own . . ." ". . . put a spy in their midst . . ."

If these were the rebels, was there already a spy in their midst?

She ran her fingers through her short-cropped hair. Until she knew that every single one of these people was to be trusted, she would continue to be a boy. Her name was still Leon.

Cautiously, she parted the curtain.

Before her was a kitchen of rough wooden surfaces lit by the golden light of early morning. It was bustling with the activity and voices of at least two dozen girls and young women, chopping, grinding, kneading, cooking. Some, sharing tasks, worked companionably shoulder to shoulder. But as one after another of the room's occupants noticed the face at the door, they fell silent. Leora had the distinct impression that the discussions had been about her.

She was surprised by their faces. Some were familiar

sorts of faces; others were brown, like the del Valles'; a few were a startling ebony.

But none of them had red hair.

"Well, good morning." The silence was broken by a young woman with freckles and curly jet black hair. "I'm Nell." It was the voice from the dream.

She moved forward with what she hoped was a boyish stride. "I'm Leon," she said, gripping Nell's outstretched hand with as strong a squeeze as she could muster.

Nell winced in surprise, then grinned. "And this is Cassie," she said, indicating a slight, angular young woman standing by the table.

"I remember," said Leora, thinking of her dream. Then she blushed, because of course they had never met.

"So you were *awake*," Cassie said, with a look of deepening suspicion.

"No," Leora said. "I was dreaming."

Cassie raised an eyebrow. She did not offer her hand but turned her back and began her task of slicing the biggest loaf of bread Leora had ever seen.

"Do you know you're on an island, Leon?" said Nell when she had finished introducing Leora to the others and turned her attention to the potatoes that sizzled over an open fireplace.

So this *was* the island. Which meant that these must indeed be the rebels.

But where was Reba?

"We brought you here last night," Nell went on. "You were at the landing," she added, her voice inviting an explanation.

Leora didn't know what to say. Was one of them a spy? Dare she let them know that the redheaded Reba Moran might still be alive? Or that Reba's sister, Leora Moran, condemned to the Institute, was also alive and free?

"I'm looking for my sister," she blurted out at last, deciding to keep the details to herself.

"Is she here, Leon?" Nell asked softly after a moment's silence.

"Is this everybody?" asked Leora.

"This is everybody."

With a sinking heart, Leora looked at each in turn. It was not as if she could have missed a head of red hair!

"Absolutely everybody?"

"Absolutely everybody."

"Then she's not," Leora said miserably.

"What's your sister's name?"

"Millie," Leora lied in a mumble, avoiding sympathetic glances by looking at the ground.

Not even in the darkest corner of her mind had Leora believed that she would fail to find Reba. Tears dimmed her vision. She was only vaguely aware of the returning bustle and chatter. Someone pressed her down onto a bench at the table.

Soon everyone was sitting and a plate had been placed before her. Faced with a generous serving of the eagerly awaited potatoes, she found she was no longer hungry. Her mouth was dry. The food slid with difficulty past a rising lump in her throat and proceeded to stick in her chest.

She was tucked tightly between two girls not much older than herself. One, named Maya, had features that reminded her of the del Valles. The other, named Bree, had skin darker than a barka nut. When Leora's tears had brimmed over and were plopping one at a time onto her potatoes, it was Bree who suggested softly that their visitor might like to explore the island.

Grateful for the chance to cry in private, Leora was about to stand when Cassie voiced dissent. "We have no reason to trust him, do we?"

"But, Cassie," responded an older girl named Zena. "There's nothing secret out there but the island itself."

"And *that's* not a secret anymore, is it?" said Cassie reproachfully.

"He'll do no harm," said Nell.

Her statement brought murmured assent, and Cassie turned abruptly away.

"Go," Bree said, nudging her. "We'll save your breakfast."

Leora stumbled clumsily off the bench and fled for the door.

"Just keep to the side of the island on the open sea, the side of the rising sun. So that you can't be seen from land," Bree called after her.

But Leora was no longer paying attention. Running out the door, she escaped gladly from the eyes and ears of strangers. Her feet tangled in the long-fingered juniper as she leaned into the wind and stumbled toward the hazy brightness of the morning sky.

Eventually, she found herself atop a stark cliff of rock, from which a slate gray sea spread out, growing paler and paler until it blended seamlessly with a white sky. The desolate scene was accented by the call of crows, their shrill voices rebuking her for her invasion of their turf.

Yesterday, from the Dragon's Tongue, the island view had offered a promise of beauty and hope. Now, the limitless ocean spread out and dissolved into nowhere. She had arrived at her destination, and there was nothing. How could she have thought that she could find Reba? Reba was dead. Killed by the guards. Or by the birmbas, just like they said.

If it weren't for her hand, she'd be home in Village Three, secure in Norie's familiar kitchen. She shoved her hand deep into her cape pocket, as if she might be able to bury it out of existence.

Unexpectedly, the tips of her webbed finger encountered a surface, hard and smooth. It was . . . a barka nut! Reaching back into the recesses of her pocket, she discovered two more nuts.

Had these been in her pocket the night before when she had scoured the Dragon's Tongue for something—anything—to eat? No. She was sure, for much of the evening her hands had been tucked into her cape pockets for protection against the chilly sea air.

So how did the nuts get there? She rolled one of the barka nuts in her webbed hand.

Tomo.

That was it.

The dream about Tomo searching her pockets for Norie's pastries was no dream, and Tomo had not been looking for pastries.

"He was bringing me food," she said out loud, to no one in particular.

A seagull, which had been hovering before her, lit gently on an outcropping of rock.

"He brought me barka nuts because I was hungry," she said, addressing the seagull now.

"Birmbas know things like that," Leora added, as if the gull doubted her statement. "He knew that Howie would be caught in Village Fifteen. And I got mad at him for it!"

She held the barka nuts against her cheek.

"He must have hid when Cassie and Nell came. And I didn't even get to tell him I was sorry."

The gull looked as if he might be considering this when Leora was distracted by a sudden brightening of the landscape. The sun, peeking through an opening in the fog, turned the sea into a mirror of light. The sleeping island came alive as its stubbly fur of glowing crowberry was transformed into a shaggy coat of vivid green.

"Tomo might still be at the Dragon's Tongue," Leora said. "Maybe I can see him there if I go to the other side."

Her feet were already picking their way over the pink rocky outcropping toward the island's landward edge.

Suspected

FACING LAND and gazing across the choppy water, Leora could make out the sheer twin chasms of the Dragon's Tongue, the fierce collision of water with rock. Although the fog had lifted, the sunlight and the promising patch of blue sky had disappeared, leaving an unyielding expanse of dismal gray.

Tomo was nowhere to be seen.

Well, she could hardly have expected that he would be standing there waiting for her to appear. She shaded her eyes against the dull glare of sky, scanning the distant textured layer of evergreen.

Although her feet were planted firmly on the island's rough rock, in her mind Leora was other places: She was creeping out of Norie's kitchen without even a good-bye; she was trying to hold her ground as Wiggala, eyes forlorn, disappeared into the woods on Mama

Birmba's back; she was dashing down the hill to Village Fifteen leaving Tomo, hurt and scolded, at her back; and finally, she was rushing back up the same hill to the woods, leaving Howie and the del Valles behind.

Well, she had left them all for nothing.

If Reba wasn't a rebel, Leora didn't belong here. If Reba was dead, Leora didn't belong anywhere. Except in the Institute.

All that remained for her to hope for was a sighting of Tomo.

Leora was so engaged in searching the contours of the distant rocks that the crash of brush behind her came as a total surprise.

"Hey! What are you *doing?*"

Leora spun around in dismay. It was the girl named Zena, her face angry and alarmed.

"Get away from here!" Zena grabbed her by the shoulder, pushing her urgently back into the brush. "You better get up to the house. Now!"

Leora wondered what she might have done wrong. Then the words she had heard, but not paid any attention to, came back to her. About staying away from the landward side. Of course. That would be important.

As Leora stumbled back under cover, she could feel her last thread of connection to the mainland stretching taut and breaking with a snap.

The rebels had been suspicious of her in the first place. Now what would they think?

"Who were you looking for, Leon?"

The question came from Nell. Half a dozen of the rebels were gathered about her in the sleeping room. Faces that had so recently borne a look of open curiosity and sympathy now appeared closed and set.

"It's obvious, isn't it?" said Cassie. "He was sent to betray us. We should have left him there on the rocks."

"He was looking for something. Watching for someone on the mainland. I'm sure of it," Zena said.

"Who were you looking for, Leon?" Nell asked again, her voice grim. "We have to know."

"I thought Tomo was there," Leora mumbled at last.

"Tomo?"

"A birmba," Leora said weakly.

The islanders exchanged glances.

"Three of the birmbas are my friends," Leora protested. "I freed one of them, a baby, from the basement of my house. Then I had to escape." They were staring at her in disbelief, but she plowed on. "One of them, named Tomo, protected me all the way to Village Fifteen. He found water for me to drink. And he fed me. He made nests for me to sleep in at night."

Leora pushed the words out faster and faster. "Tomo tried to protect my friend from getting captured in the village and he knew it was going to happen and I got mad at him for it," she ended, fighting tears.

They looked at her, speechless.

Only Cassie found her voice. "And just how did you find your way to the Dragon's Tongue? I suppose your birmba friend led you there."

"Go easy, Cassie." Nell put a restraining hand on Cassie's shoulder. "Leon is . . . upset and . . . confused."

Leora saw that one of the rebels was tapping her head. First they thought she was a spy. Now they thought she was crazy.

"How *did* you find your way to the Dragon's Tongue?" Nell asked, clearly holding out little hope for a sane answer.

"Someone told me about it. Then I found the way myself."

Cassie laughed. "And I'm the queen of the nightingales!"

"Leon," Nell continued, speaking slowly and gently, as one might talk to a three-year-old, "do you think you can tell me who . . . told you the way?"

"It was Lex," Leora answered. "He was in Village Fifteen. Though he came from a village to the north, from the tribe of the People of the First Light."

"Not Lex!" Zena paled.

Leora noticed that Zena's stern features were similar to Lex's.

"Do you think the guards have captured him?" Bree asked Zena. "And got the information out of him?"

"Lex would die before he told!" Zena said staunchly. "The boy's lying."

"But if the guards gave Lex's name to Leon . . . they must know about Lex."

"Oh noooo," Zena moaned.

"No!" Leora insisted. "They don't know about him. Lex is fine. He's organizing a patrol to keep the guards from burning the village."

"Burning the village?"

"Yes. I told him that the guards were going to burn the village."

"Ah, yes. A little birmba told you that would happen," Cassie muttered.

"No. I . . . I . . . I saw it. Like a dream . . . except . . . except I wasn't asleep."

Nell looked surprised, and studied her hard for just a moment before turning away.

Cassie shook her head as if at last it was all too outlandish even for sarcasm.

After that, they talked about her as if she weren't even there.

"What shall we do now?" Bree asked glumly. "Are they on to us?"

"If they knew where we were, they would just come and destroy us."

"Not if they thought they could plant a spy and learn something about the entire movement first."

"Yes!" cried Leora. "They *are* planning on planting a spy! I heard them from up in a tree. Unless . . ." *Unless they already have*, she finished the sentence in her mind, carefully examining the faces around her.

The conversation continued as if she were not only invisible, but mute.

"He's crazy," Zena said.

"Crazy like a fox," said Cassie, eyeing Leora with contempt.

"Maybe he escaped from the Institute," Zena suggested.

The Institute! At least they didn't know about her hand. Beneath her cape, it felt limp and useless now, like a broken wing.

"Well, either way," said Nell, "we can't take him back. We'll just have to keep him here until . . . we make our move."

"We'll have to keep close watch," said Zena. "Even if he means no harm, we can't have him waving at the mainland at his imaginary friends."

Nell nodded. "Bree," she said, "why don't you take the first watch. And get him something more to eat. If it's true he escaped from the Institute, he might have been wandering around alone in the woods for days.

"It's a wonder the birmbas didn't get him."

Crazy

LEORA STARED out the narrow window of the sleeping room, watching a tiny rectangle of island terrain appear and disappear in the fog. Had two days passed? Or more? She felt as if she were sleepwalking.

It was obvious that the more she tried to explain herself, the crazier the rebels thought she was. Maybe she *was* crazy.

"Bree," said Nell. "It's clearing up. Would you mind collecting some chana berries for me? I'll be heading to Village Fifteen, and I'd better have some dye before I go.

"And, Leon," she added. "Maybe you'd like to go along with Bree and get yourself some fresh air."

Leora was sorry to hear that Nell would be gone. It wasn't that the rebels were unkind to her. They seemed to have accepted that she was harmless. But now they acted as if she were witless. Only Nell acted as if Leora was actually capable of speech.

Leora tagged behind Bree. The air was rich and sweet with the smell of the sea, and, as the fog lifted, the vivid blue of the opening sky stood out against the mossy green of the wild crowberry. The beauty stirred something within her, and before long, as they made their way through low-branching scrub, she broke her silence to ask Bree the name of first one plant and then another.

Bree seemed pleased by Leora's curiosity. Soon she was sharing all she knew: about the twining purple beach pea, the pungent juniper berry, and the multicolored lichens. And best of all, the rugosas: the wild pink beach roses that had a perfume sweeter than the smell of the sea. Clearly Bree had a deep love and knowledge of every growing thing. Her dark eyes were bright with excitement as she looked out over the coral pink rock, the ocean, the dizzying breadth of sky. Leora found herself memorizing her companion's face.

They had been silent for some minutes when Bree spoke. "Leon, do you feel really uncomfortable? Being . . . different?"

Leora, stunned, felt a wave of shame, and thrust her hand deeper into her pocket.

"I mean," Bree went on, "it must be hard being the only boy."

Leora almost laughed in relief. She wanted to tell

Bree the truth. But she knew that it might make the rebels wonder why she had lied in the first place, and reawaken their early suspicion that she was a spy. Besides, she reminded herself, until she could be assured that there was *not* a spy planted amid them, she had to keep her own identity a secret.

"When I first came here," Bree said, "I was the different one. I was the first one here with black skin."

Leora turned to her in surprise. "Black?" she said.

"Hadn't you noticed?" Bree smiled.

"Well," Leora said, "I thought more . . . brown. Like a barka nut."

Bree laughed. "Well, at least I'm not a mutation like a barka nut."

Leora flushed, and curled the fingers of her left hand tightly in her pocket.

"Leon, you'd never seen anyone like me before, had you?"

Leora shook her head.

"Well, no one else here had either. In the village I came from, everyone was like me. Only the guards were different—with their white skin.

"My people really came from far across the ocean," Bree went on. "Brought here in chains. For over two hundred years, my people were owned by the white people here."

"Owned?" said Leora in horror. Leora looked at Bree,

trying to fathom it. Her hand seemed to understand at least some of it. It wanted to reach out and touch Bree and make it all not true.

"Things were just beginning to change when the Disaster came. My great-great-grandfather was the captain of the whole navy," Bree said proudly. "But after the Disaster, when the Rulers took over, they divided people up and put them in separate villages."

"Why?"

"That's easy," Bree said. "If the Rulers keep us separate, and if everything that is true is forbidden-to-tell, they can control us with our own ignorance. They can make each village believe bad things about those in other villages. They can make us hate one another. So that we'll never get together. Never join up against them."

Leora remembered Wilfert, at the dinner table so long ago, telling Tanette about the brown-skinned people in Village Fifteen; "secretive and disobedient," he had called them. And her stepfather, the governor, in a hushed voice, talking to Wilfert about "mutual suspicion." How little she had understood at the time!

"What did they tell your village about . . . us . . .?" Leora asked. She was unaccustomed to thinking of herself as belonging to any "us." "I mean about the . . . white villagers."

" 'Mean and selfish,' " Bree said without hesitation.

"The only white people I ever knew before I came here were the guards. And they certainly fit that description! It took me a while to trust anyone here. It's hard being the only different one—until you find out that everybody's different—so, really, everybody's the same."

Again Leora could feel her hand wanting to reach out, to touch Bree's delicate dark hand with her own webbed fingers.

They walked together in silence. As they descended into a gentle valley, they came upon a small group of the rebels, their backs bent, pulling huge rocks from the soil. A second group was planting dozens of tiny fruit trees in the newly cleared earth. Farther on, three girls pounded and twisted a pile of calpa vine into rope, their hands bleeding from the task.

Leora knew that the islanders had been at work since sunup, and that they would continue work till sundown. Occasionally they stopped to confer with one another, but there were few smiles, and no laughter. She could see that it was not an easy life, scraping a living from the shallow island soil.

Like a sleepwalker waking, Leora found herself wondering about their plans. How did two dozen young women hope to mount a rebellion? How many allies like Lex and the del Valles could they have on land? If they planned a *mutiny*, as Howie called it, when would it be?

Even though she had not found Reba, she suddenly realized that whatever the rebels' plan might be, she wanted to be a part of it.

"Why do you plant fruit trees?" Leora asked, with a new curiosity. "Won't it be years before they bear fruit?"

"It will be years before we leave the island," said Bree, matter-of-factly.

"But I thought . . ." She realized that she had been imagining that the rebels would be abandoning the island within the season. To . . . do whatever it was they were going to do.

"It will be a long time from now, Leon," Bree said. "We can't hope to succeed until we have lots of supporters in each of the villages. And it's hard to do that because the birmbas make it difficult to get to the villages.

"Later on," Bree continued, "the big challenge will be for the villagers to save up enough food to get through a season. The guards have control of the food, and the first thing they'd do is try to starve the people out."

Leora heard the sound of Howie's shears in her hair, and the sound of his voice as he extracted the promise from her—the promise that she would go ahead, without him if necessary, and find the rebels. Find them to bring them two pieces of critical information: that the birmbas were friendly; and that the new-species could be safely eaten.

Thoughtfully, Leora followed Bree up a slope into an expanse of tiny-leaved chana berry bushes. Shoulder to shoulder they began plunking handfuls of the hard little berries into Bree's bucket. When Leora crushed them between her fingers, she saw that they left a deep, dark stain. She could see why they would be good for dye.

"Do many of the new-species grow on the island?" Leora asked carefully, rolling a bunch of chana berries in the palm of her hand.

"All the new-species—nitta berries, chana berries, calpa vine. If it's inedible, it grows here."

"Bree," said Leora slowly. "Do I seem crazy to you?"

Bree looked embarrassed. "Well . . ."

Leora was silent. She feared she was about to risk the trust of their short-lived friendship.

"Bree, I came here all the way from Village Three. I survived because the birmbas took care of me. I promise you, they're completely harmless so long as you don't point a gun at them. And I promise you, the new-species *are* edible. I know because I ate them."

A look of dismay came over Bree's face. There was a long pause. Finally Bree said, "I have work to do."

Leora felt a tightening around her heart. Was this how Tomo felt when he had been unable to communicate to her and Howie the danger that lay ahead in Village Fifteen?

Well. She might not be able to convince them that

the birmbas were harmless. But she could certainly convince them that the new-species were edible.

As Bree immersed herself in her work, Leora sidled toward a darker patch of green where the bushes were clustered with the familiar deep purple nitta berries. With her back to Bree, she plucked and pocketed several handfuls. She would show them the berries were safe to eat. It was only a matter of waiting for a moment when she had plenty of witnesses.

Nitta Berries

WITH THE FINGERTIPS of her right hand, Leora explored the firm, plump berries that waited in the recesses of her pocket.

The rebels crouched in a circle at the center of the sleeping room, leaning against one another for warmth. Their faces—pale, brown, and ebony—were illuminated by the dancing candlelight and united in their serious intensity. It was as if the young women themselves were woven together like the great striped blanket that hung on the wall. The feeling in the room reminded her of the feeling in the del Valles' kitchen. It was the feeling of a family. She would have liked to be a part of it.

Still wet from being washed, Nell's wild hair was smooth, sleeked down, and blacker than ever. She reminded Leora of a panther. But only in appearance. In manner she was gentle, attentive, and fair-minded. Leora knew if she were alone with Nell, even her webbed hand would feel safe and comfortable being out in the open.

Although there seemed to be no established leader among the rebels, Leora noticed that again and again it was Nell whom everyone looked to for the final word. But even Nell was having a hard time moderating tonight's discussion. It had become a heated debate. How would they know when the time was right to act? And when was that likely to be?

Leora stroked the hidden berries.

"I know we're all willing to take great risks," Zena was saying. "But if we try to rush things and get killed by the birmbas in the process, it will take even longer."

"If only we could lay our hands on some of the guards' guns to defend ourselves from the birmbas. . . ."

"If the birmbas were harmless," Leora asked suddenly, "and we could get easily between villages to recruit, could the revolution happen sooner?"

The rebels seemed as surprised as if the teapot had spoken. Leora saw Bree shifting uncomfortably now in her seat.

Cassie groaned.

"Yes, Leon," Nell answered in a level voice. "Then it might only take one year to recruit and train people, and another year to save and hide away enough food."

"What if you had enough food already?" Leora continued.

Nell hesitated, then nodded slowly. "That would be extremely helpful, Leon."

Leora, fingering the nitta berries in her pocket, gathered her courage. She stood up in the center of the circle, feeling their eyes upon her.

"Well," she said, her voice sounding loud and unfamiliar in her own ears, "I know I can't prove to you that the birmbas are harmless." She collected a fistful of berries. "But I *can* prove to you that the new-species are edible."

"Nitta berries," she said simply, displaying them in her palm. Then she crammed them into her mouth. For a few moments, the rebels simply gaped. It was Nell who reached her first, clapping her arms around her and pulling her to the ground.

"Oh, Leon! What have you done?"

"Don't worry. They're not poisonous," Leora insisted. She was surprised to see Nell so upset.

"It must have been when we gathered the chana berries." Bree lamented. "I wasn't paying attention to him. On the way over there we talked about plants and things. He seemed so . . . normal. But then he started telling me that the birmbas are friendly, and that you can eat the new-species. I should never have taken my eyes off him!"

"They're not poisonous!" Leora repeated, her voice

growing louder. "Don't you see?" she said, standing up in her excitement. "It's all part of things being forbidden-to-know. The Rulers keep us ignorant about each other. You know that! They also keep us ignorant about the plants, the animals, and probably other things, too."

It had only occurred to Leora as she spoke that the Rulers might already know that the plants weren't poisonous. But if so, did the guards know?

The rebels stared at her dumbly. Even Nell seemed too distraught by what Leora had done to pay any attention to her words.

"We know that nitta berries are poisonous," said Cassie, clearly eager to comfort Nell. "But we don't know that they're deadly, do we?"

"But they're *not* poisonous," Leora protested, one last time. "If I'm alive tomorrow, you'll have to believe it." She wanted to add, *and you'll have to believe that the birmbas aren't dangerous either.*

Throughout the remainder of the meeting, Leora caught many worried glances aimed at her. The rebels seemed surprised and confused by her continued good health.

She in turn was watching them. Each spoke with dogged resolution about going forward. They spoke with passion, but none of them spoke with hope.

Leora wondered: Would Maya, and Zena, and Bree each fall before the gun of a guard? Die for one another? Die for all the people of Maynor? Like the del Valles, the rebels were part of a family. But this was a family with roots as deep and wide as Maynor itself.

She closed her eyes. She imagined her hand was moving. It was sketching a throng of people in the old Town Hall. They were people of all ages, who had traveled freely from all directions, who had different voices of differing opinions.

She was imagining Howie and Norie within the crowd, when she heard Zena speaking, and found herself again the center of attention. "If something were going to happen to him, wouldn't it have happened by now?"

❧

By bedtime, most of the rebels seemed to believe that Leora was out of danger. But Leora awoke in the night to the touch of a hand on her forehead, and found Nell leaning over her.

"I'm fine," said Leora.

"I'm glad of that, Leon." Nell straightened up, clearly relieved. "You had me very worried."

But still Nell did not go to bed. Leora watched as the young woman paced in the darkness, pausing to look down first at one sleeper and then another.

It was as if the solitude and darkness had ripped away whatever hope and comfort she wrapped about herself in the daylight. Leora could sense the depth of her concern about the dangerous times that lay ahead.

Then there was a gust of cold as Nell slipped out the door into the night.

Leora's hand stirred. She climbed out from under her covers and crept silently after her. The wind brought the sound and smell of the sea, and pulled low-hanging clouds quickly over a full moon. In the distance she spotted Nell standing on a crest of rock, her back to the compound, looking eastward toward the moon's veiled light.

Leora felt the energy coursing through her hand. As she had at the del Valles', she could feel that beyond her hand lay a force of alarming proportions. Although she might disbelieve it in the morning, at this minute she was certain that unless they connected with this force, there would be no victory for the rebels.

She moved softly toward Nell.

Nell turned, her face distraught in the moonlight.

"You don't have to worry, Nell," Leora said. "The hermit thrush *will* sing again."

"Oh, Leon," Nell said, then reached out and wrapped an arm around Leora's shoulder. "How could you know what I was thinking? If you can read the future as well as you just read my thoughts . . . well . . . then . . . the hermit thrush will definitely sing again."

Warning

"WILL YOU be bringing anyone back?" Zena was asking Nell as Leora rose out of sleep.

"I don't know yet. Mostly we'll be trying to make contacts in Village Fifteen—recruiting more people to spread the word within the village."

Leora sat bolt upright.

It was that word *recruit*. She was perched in the night nest with Wiggala and Mama Birmba. A voice was rising from below. ". . . *let her recruit one of our own . . . betray her own cause before we take her prisoner. . . .*"

"No!" Leora said emphatically. "Don't go!"

"Don't worry, Leon," Nell said kindly. "Zena and Bree will take good care of you."

Nell and Cassie continued stowing their packs. "This could be our most useful trip yet," Nell was saying to

Zena. "There's a rumor that one of the guards is prepared to begin supplying us with information."

As she said this, Leora felt as if the shadow of a great cloud were passing over them. It was followed by an unpleasant feeling in the bottom of her stomach. It was a familiar sick feeling. It was the way she felt . . . around Wilfert!

"You can't go!" Leora said even more insistently. "Your contact. He's a spy!" Her fingers tingled.

"Yes, Leon," Nell said. "You could call him that. But he will be *our* spy. Working for us against them. Don't worry."

"No! He's a spy for them!" The tingling in her fingers intensified.

"Don't worry," Bree assured Nell. "We'll keep an eye on Leon. He'll be okay."

Leora grabbed her bag and snatched out a piece of paper and a charcoal stick. Keeping her fingers close together, and hunching over the paper to conceal her hand, she began to draw, her fingers whisking fast as lightning over the rough surface of the paper.

First the ferretlike eyes. Then the receding chin. The sharp nose. And finally the tense, puppetlike body clothed in the square-shouldered guardsman's uniform. When Wilfert's likeness was complete, she thrust the page toward Cassie and Nell.

"This is him," she said.

"Look at this!" Cassie exclaimed. "Some imagination!"

"It's not imaginary!" Leora protested. "It's real! He's a guard, all right. But he plans to make you betray all you've done. Whatever you do, don't let him know you're rebels. It would be the end of everything!"

Nell studied the picture carefully. "You're quite an artist, Leon. And that's a wonderful gift." She looked hard at Leora. Leora was sure she was remembering their nighttime encounter. But all she said was, "There are some magnificent outlooks on the island here. Zena and Bree will take you around, if you want to draw."

"You must have nothing to do with him!" Leora said urgently. "You have to promise!"

"Nell," said Bree. "He *was* right about the nitta berries."

Again Nell studied the drawing, and again she turned to Leora. She looked as if she were trying to see through her, into something beyond her and invisible. Finally she sighed and tossed her head, as if to shake off a memory or a dream.

"Well, Leon. I will promise. If I see anyone who looks like this, I'll have nothing to do with him."

One of the rebels laughed softly.

Leora was sure Nell hadn't meant to be poking fun at her. But the extra kindness in her voice left Leora worried that her warning had been given in vain.

Leora refused to be put off. "Cassie?" she said. "Do

you promise, too?" She knew she was pushing their patience, and Cassie was not a person to push.

"Leon," Cassie groaned. "It is unlikely that I will ever have the misfortune of being confronted by any of the demons of your wild imagination." She walked to the window. "The tide is close to full. We have no more time to waste."

As they left, Nell turned back and added, "The Fifteeners are making us a new boat. It's time we started repairing the dock. I'm afraid it was weakened by that last storm."

Then they were gone.

Leora shivered. She had the sensation that there was some other warning that she should have given them. She didn't know what it was. She only knew it was a matter of life and death.

Premonition

THE CLINK OF CUTLERY at breakfast was unaccompanied by the usual eager chatter. Nell and Cassie's departure had left the rebels in a sober mood.

Leora looked at the faces around her. She was glad about one thing. If the guards were only now about to plant a spy, it must mean that they had not yet managed to do it. Which meant that, within this family of rebels she was coming to care about, there were no traitors.

Her hand, she realized, had known this all along.

She decided that the time had come to talk to Nell. To tell her about Reba. And about herself. Of course there was no reason now that the rest of them couldn't be trusted with the information. But Nell was the one she wanted to confide in.

I'll tell her, she thought, when she returns.

Then something inside of her added, *if* she returns.

"Leon! Are you in a daze? Wake up." Bree jostled her. "Maya was just saying that we should collect a few buckets of nitta berries, and she'll make us some corn cakes with nitta berry jam for dinner."

The rebels that morning had been only too happy to acknowledge that they had misjudged her. She looked around now to discover that she was the center of a good deal of cheery attention and a rapidly improving mood. She guessed that the prospect of expanding their immediate food supply had something to do with it. But it was clear that underneath their pleasure was a new confidence in their overall plan. Now they could rest assured that the people of Maynor would not be threatened by starvation during their revolution.

But how about the more critical fact: that the birmbas were friendly. Would the rebels now believe her about that?

As if reading her mind, Bree whispered in her ear, "Don't say anything again about the birmbas. Let them get used to one thing at a time."

Leora nodded in surprise. Then smiled. As she looked around, she saw something in the room she had not glimpsed since she had been on the island: hope.

⁘

"You have to understand about Cassie," said Bree as the two of them cleared up after breakfast. "About why she's so suspicious."

Bree paused. Leora stowed the earthenware cups on a shelf. She was reminded of how Norie might begin to tell her a tale and felt a pang of longing for Norie and her kitchen.

"Cassie grew up in the next village over from Village Fifteen," Bree began. "It was Cassie's family that took in Nell after her parents died. When the two of them weren't much older than you are now, they started getting interested in the way things were in the Before Time. Talking to old-timers and all. And slowly they cooked up the plan to start a new place for people who were against the Rulership."

Leora stopped cleaning up, all attention on Bree.

"There were two others in on it with them. One was Cassie's brother. The other was a friend of his, a boy who lived next door. And the boys wanted to be part of it—to leave, with Cassie and Nell. But Cassie said no, they would be missed. Because they were boys, you know, and already working under the guards, tending crops and all."

Bree settled down at the kitchen table, Leora beside her.

"So Nell and Cassie left, and came here to start all of this. And the next thing Cassie knows, her brother's friend has told all and betrayed them. The guards can't lay their hands on Cassie, so they get their revenge by taking her brother and putting him in the Institute."

"The Institute?" Leora whispered. "But he wasn't . . . defective . . . or anything. Was he?"

Bree looked hard at Leora. "Are you all right? You look pale."

Leora nodded.

"No. He wasn't defective," Bree continued. "But he did have a temper to beat the band. That was all the excuse they needed.

"Now her brother has been in the Institute for a third of his life. And Cassie, she's eaten up her innards with worry and guilt. She thinks that if she hadn't been so foolish as to trust the neighbor boy, her brother would be safe at home. Or here with her by now. I think that's part of why she's so ready to mistrust you. Because she hates herself for having placed trust in the wrong person before. And a boy, to boot, about your age."

Leora had forgotten that Bree thought she was a boy. "Bree . . ." she began.

But Bree continued. "So you see, if anyone were to betray the rebels now, she'd *never* be able to rescue her brother."

"Don't worry, Bree. When it's time, I'll help Cassie get her brother out of the Institute." Leora surprised herself with this last statement.

"Oh, Leon!" said Bree, giving her a friendly nudge. "You are a bundle of surprises. Come. Let's go see how they're coming with the dock."

As they walked, Bree pointed out her favorite spots.

"You should have brought your paper, Leon," she said as they marveled at the grace of a wind-bent spruce. "Do you think you could teach me to draw?"

Leora mumbled. She wondered if Bree would be willing to be her friend if she knew about her hand.

A picture began forming in her mind. It was not of the island's rugged beauty, though, but of Wilfert, disguised and waiting. It was strange that it was Nell whom Wilfert would be trying to entrap in the village today. In her dream in the forest, it had been Reba.

But the closer she and Bree got to the roar of the sea, the more this fear was overshadowed by an even darker premonition. It wasn't the way she'd felt this morning, thinking about Wilfert. It was something larger, dark, and empty.

From a low bluff near the dock, they leaned into a rising wind, listening to the rhythmic whoosh of the water against the island's rocky edge. Below, half a dozen of the young women, up to their waists in the heaving sea, struggled to beach a great tree trunk, a gift from some distant shore.

"The trees on the island are too small and scrubby to be useful for the dock," said Bree. "The dock's made entirely from wood from the sea."

Below, the women worked together, pushing, pulling, and heaving. Clinging to the trunk, they looked like parts of a single creature, a giant water beetle navigating the swells.

As Leora and Bree watched, the sea sucked back forcefully and swiftly, twisting and pulling the log, and the women along with it. Leora gasped as two of them disappeared briefly under the water's surface.

"Do you swim?" asked Bree, as the women resurfaced and rode the trunk safely onto the beach.

"Swim?" It had never occurred to her that anything but a fish could swim.

"Well, Cassie will make sure that you learn. She insists we all do. Though she's never managed to convince Nell to learn how."

Bree's statement precipitated another wave of dread, a terrible tugging feeling, as if she were being pulled down into a whirlpool of infinite darkness.

She forced herself to put the feeling aside. Then, keeping her hand concealed as best she could, she spent the rest of the day helping the rebels gather calpa vine to be pounded into rope for the repair of the dock. By sundown, most of them had bleeding hands from the task of beating and twisting the scratchy stalks.

Tomorrow they would begin the task of fortifying the pier. They wanted to have it in good condition by the time Nell and Cassie returned. But tonight, they seemed in a mood to celebrate.

"Here's to Leon," said Bree, when they were all quite

stuffed with Maya's corn cakes and nitta berry jam.

"Yes, yes," cried Maya. "And don't you think we should toast him with a split-cup of blueberry cordial?"

This idea met with enthusiastic shouts of approval, though Leora wasn't sure whether it was the toasting part or the blueberry cordial part that was so popular.

It turned out that a *split-cup* meant that every two people shared a cup. Leora shared hers with Bree, the cup going back and forth between them for the tiniest of sips, prolonging the enjoyment of the potent sweet brew.

Maybe it was the cordial, but Leora soon felt drowsy. And divided. Almost as if she were living in two worlds at once. One of the worlds was filled with the rich smells of cooking, her jolly companions, and the comfort of Bree's shoulder next to hers. The other was filled with the darkness that swept over her again without warning, like a tidal wave rising out of a placid sea.

"How about potato and calpa root stew?"

"How about nitta berry wine?" The ideas for recipes made of new-species had taken on a rowdy tone.

"Yes! Yes! Let's make it all tomorrow, in time for Cassie and Nell. They'll be hungry enough from their mission."

"It's too late to make it for them," Leora said abruptly, finding herself very awake indeed. Her heartbeat had quickened. "They're coming back tonight."

Bree didn't have time to contradict this statement.

A chill blast of wind accompanied the sound of the opening door.

It was Cassie.

Something in her face silenced the celebration. Leora strained her eyes behind her for the sight of Nell. But she already knew.

Cassie was alone.

Accused

"WHERE'S NELL?" cried Zena in alarm.

"Don't worry," snapped Cassie. "She's on her way. The Fifteeners made us a new boat. She's in it. It's just slower than our old one. She's ten minutes behind me." Cassie slammed the door and strode in. She glowered at Leora.

"What's wrong, Cassie?" one of them asked.

"Everything's wrong. We saw him."

"Saw who?"

"The guard in the picture. The defector. The one who was going to give us the inside information. Leon knew who he was, all right. He drew him to a tee."

"So did you talk to him?"

"No," growled Cassie. "Nell said she'd promised. She said the boy knew things."

"Knew things?"

"Oh, who knows what she meant," said Cassie, staring at Leora. "All I know is, the boy's a spy."

"How do you know? What makes you so sure?"

"How else would he know what one of theirs looked like? They must already have suspected that this guard might come to our side. The boy's hoodwinked Nell.

"And now," Cassie continued, her voice rising in irritation, "who knows if we'll ever get another chance with the guard. If he is under suspicion, he could be killed at any time. And there goes our chance!"

"But, Cassie!" said Bree. "If he was under suspicion, they might have been watching him. They could have caught you and Nell just for talking to him."

Cassie's face clouded. "I don't know what to think. Except I do know the boy's dividing us. When have we ever fought, Nell and I? Never! The whole of Maynor is at stake, and this boy is splitting us up. We can't afford to trust him."

"Cassie," Bree argued. "You always see spies everywhere. Remember you even thought Zena was a spy. It's not Leon's fault you left your brother to be taken to the Institute!"

"Bree! Stop!" said Zena. "Cassie's right. We shouldn't let this divide us."

"At least give him a chance to explain himself," said Bree. "He *was* right about the nitta berries, you know."

Zena nodded. "Leon," she said at last. "How *did* you find us here?"

Now that they believed her about the nitta berries, would they believe her about the rest? Where to begin?

In rapid succession, Leora saw in her mind the stony enclose of Village Three, and the veery beyond the gate. She saw Wiggala's furry form and trusting gaze. She saw Tomo, large and sulky; and Tomo eating berry tarts; and finally, Tomo glowering balefully at her as she parted from him.

As if in a dream, she heard Howie's jovial voice: *Well, I'll be scuttled*; and Yano: *A girl*; and Margarita: *A sister*.

"Out of darkness into light," Leora said, unaware she had said it out loud until she looked around at a sea of very puzzled faces.

"He's getting strange again," someone muttered.

"Don't you see!" Cassie exploded. "He's *pretending* to be crazy. Every time we ask him hard questions he does his crazy act. He's sane enough all the rest of the time. Well, isn't he?" She looked around for support, and Leora knew that once again Cassie had scored a point.

Leora didn't know what the rebels would do with her now. They'd imprison her, at the very least. They might not want to, but as Cassie had said, the whole of Maynor was at stake.

She reached for the familiar contours of her locket. She wondered for the hundredth time what the words in the lockets meant. Why, if Grand Nan could tell the future, would she have made two lockets, for . . . nothing?

Again there came a sensation of something tugging at her from the darkness. She felt increasingly dizzy, and the locket between her fingertips felt as if it might dissolve. The longer she held it, the more she knew that something was wrong. Very wrong. And it had to do with Nell.

"Hey!" yelled Cassie, with such suddenness and fury that Leora was startled into snapping the slender silver chain of her locket, leaving the crescent shining in the candlelight on the table.

"It's Nell's locket!" Cassie continued in outrage. "The one she carries secret messages in when we go to town. He's a spy and a *thief*!"

"Oh, Leon," moaned Bree.

"It's mine," Leora said, cupping her hand over the silver crescent on the table.

"Leon," Bree said softly from behind her, placing her hand on her shoulder. "Let it go. It belongs to Nell."

"No! It's mine!"

Her mind was spinning. Was she going crazy? The room had grown unbearably close.

"How did he get it, anyway?" Maya asked. "Wasn't Nell wearing it today in town, Cassie?"

"Apparently not," said Cassie, reaching for the locket.

"That locket is not yours!" Leora shouted, jumping out of her seat. "And if Nell wears one about her neck, it is not hers! The lockets were given to me and my sister by our Grand Nan, before we were ever born. My sister's was her special treasure. She would have given it to no one. Not to Nell. Not to anyone, ever! Where is my sister? What have you done with her?"

Overwhelmed with rage, she hurled herself at Cassie, who stood stunned into speechlessness as Leora pummeled her with more force than she had ever known she possessed.

"If you've hurt her I shall have you destroyed. The birmbas will crunch you and grind you to dust."

The swirling and darkness that had been tugging at her all day increased. Suddenly it was as if her entire body had been plunged into water as cold and wild as the sea. Her lungs cried for air, and her limbs, entangled by clothes, flailed against a sea that sucked her into its depths.

"Nell!" she cried. "She's drowning!"

And with that she was out the door into the night's dark wind.

She was scarcely aware that the others were behind her as her feet pounded toward the landing. It took her only a few moments, but it felt like forever. In her mind she had already seen what greeted her when she arrived at the sea's edge—the second boat, adrift, rising and sinking on the hills and troughs of the black sea. Empty.

She was only vaguely aware of Cassie's despairing voice howling, "Nell!" into the wind.

Leora's cape and shoes were already off as her feet left the dock and her body plunged for real into the icy darkness. The sea accepted her as if she had been swimming in it all her life, and, sure as a fish hawk and strong as a seal, she dove deep, arriving back up at the spot where Nell surfaced for what surely would have been the last time.

Struggling against the swells, Leora wrapped her left arm firmly beneath Nell's chin and held her face above the water. Through the tangle of hair, she felt Nell's head slipping perfectly into the cradle of her hand.

It was then that her webbed fingers, at last, told her all: She needed look no farther for her sister than to the still face in the crook of her arm.

Nell and Reba were one and the same.

Two Lockets

As Cassie leaned over the motionless body, pumping rhythmically, there was no sound but that of the sea. The rebels were silent.

Again and again the sea sucked out, and crashed back against the remains of the pier. The wind quieted. No one spoke. Leora's webbed hand rested on the back of her sister's neck. Please, Grand Nan, she silently begged, make it not be for nothing.

Then came a choke, and a heave—the sweetest sound she'd ever heard.

At last, Nell, coughing, pulled herself to a crouch.

"I thought it was all over," she gasped. "I could feel my sister and my Grand Nan close by."

"It was *Leon* that saved you," said Zena.

Nell reached in the darkness for Leora's hand. Leora did not withdraw it. She felt the soft, unsuspecting touch of Nell's fingers on the tender skin between her own. Nell gave a tiny gasp, and froze. Without looking at the hand in her own, she clapped her second hand over Leora's to confirm the truth. As she stared at Leora, her face was transformed first by a wave of understanding, and then by a flood of emotion.

"Oh, Leora!"

"Reba," Leora said. "My sister, Reba."

Reba's arms were around her then, and as they cried together, Leora could feel the cold, wet clothes growing warm between them.

"So you're Leora," Cassie said brusquely. "I suppose now that you've found each other, you're planning to freeze to death." And she threw her own cape around the two sisters with something suspiciously like tenderness.

Leora didn't quite remember how the rebels got the two of them back to the building, where they dried them and dressed them and wrapped them in the beautiful woven blanket from the wall.

Then, with Leora and Reba squeezing tightly into a single chair, and a new round of corn cakes heaped with nitta berry jam, they told their stories.

~

"They said you and Papa were both eaten by birmbas."

"It was a lie," said Reba, her eyes distant. "The guards shot him." Her face tensed with the awfulness of the memory. "I don't know why they did it. But they did it on purpose. I saw it. What they didn't know was that I was with him, there in the orchard."

She was silent for a few moments, then she continued. "I was playing in our special hideout under that willow. . . . Do you remember it? I stayed hidden until they left, then ran off into the woods. They must have learned later that I had been with him. And since they never found me, they probably thought I *was* eaten by the birmbas. If they had found me, they would have had to kill me. Because of what I'd seen. That's why Cassie's family had me dye my hair from the start."

"Chana berries!" said Leora.

Reba smiled. "I begged them to find a way to send you a message that I was alive. But that would have meant trusting a chopper to carry the message. And if we asked the wrong person for help, Cassie's whole family would have been killed, along with me. And you, too, if they thought we'd managed to get the message to you. For years I'd start to cry every time I thought of you!"

Reba and Leora talked into the night, the others encircling them, listening intently. It was dawn by the time Leora described the guards in Town Hall who thought she was a ghost.

As they all laughed together, Leora looked down to see that she was holding her cup of cordial with her left hand. With her fingers slightly spread, the soft webbing was clearly visible against the clay cup. She looked at Bree.

Bree's eyes were on her hand.

For a moment, Leora held her breath.

"I *knew* there was something magic about you," Bree said, looking up at Leora and grinning.

It was morning when Maya said, "So do the two lockets fit together?"

Reba slowly lifted her locket off her neck and placed it on the table next to Leora's.

"They fit, all right," said Zena, as they all marveled at the sight of the two lockets glowing in a low shaft of morning light, tucked together as snugly as two halves of a peach pit.

"Will I be able to help?" Leora finally asked. "With . . . the revolution?"

"Will you be able to help? You are our eyes, Leora," said Reba gently. "You can see outward and inward; what's visible and what's invisible. With your eyes and your hand, where there has been darkness, you will bring light."

Strategy

"THE DOVE!" cried Maya. "It's brought a message!"

Leora had been watching her friends go through their morning combat practice. The dove, which had settled on a rocky outcropping nearby, was adjusting its silvery feathers and eyeing them expectantly.

"It's from an informant," Maya explained excitedly to Leora as Reba detached a tiny roll of paper from the dove's leg.

Leora already knew about the trained mourning dove, but this was the first time she had witnessed the bird's arrival. She wondered if it was the same rosy-breasted bird who had accompanied her—was it three months ago now?—on her way from Village Fifteen to the sea.

"The informant works in the government laboratories in the capital," said Maya. "Sometimes he hears things."

The capital, Leora knew, was to the south, on the far side of the Nob River, near the Institute. These days when she thought about the Institute, it was not so much with fear for herself as with concern for Cassie's brother.

"There's trouble on the southern border," Reba was saying slowly. Zena was beside her, and the two of them were examining the message closely, surrounded by the others.

"And," said Zena, squinting at the note, "the Rulers will be pulling most of the guardsmen"— Zena's voice got loud with excitement—"*down to the South!*"

"That means," Maya explained, shaking Leora's shoulder in excitement, "that there will be fewer guards in the villages!"

"For the mutiny," said Leora.

"For the *revolution!*" said Maya, pronouncing the word with relish and raising her staff in the air for emphasis.

Something about Maya's gesture made Leora think of musket fire. She had already been worried about that. "But even if most of the guards are gone," she said, voicing her alarm, "the ones that are left will have guns! How can we possibly beat them with only . . ." Her words trailed off as she looked toward Reba's staff.

Reba, who had finished deciphering the note, grasped her own length of gnarly alder firmly with both hands. Leora was reminded of the old wild-eyed, red-haired ferocious Reba of her childhood. The memory reassured her. As if her big sister, Reba, could do *anything* with her staff.

~

"How long before . . . ?" Leora whispered anxiously to Bree as her friend took a break from combat practice.

"Days," said Bree, her eyes alive with excitement.

Part of Leora was dismayed by the news. Throughout the summer she had been spending each free moment with Reba, talking as they strolled over the soft slopes of the island, gathering berries or, more recently, the plump, sweet hips of the wild rugosa rose. It seemed that there was no end of things to share with each other.

That day Leora had seen little of Reba, who had spent the time huddled with Cassie, Zena, and the other older rebels. The island resounded with the echoes of wood meeting wood and the fierce cries of mock battle.

Feeling useless, she went to the edge of the sea with her paper and charcoal. She hoped that at least a drawing might come to her—some glimpse of the future that would help the rebels in the weeks or months that lay ahead.

But no image came to her, and she was left to contemplate the bluebells and the twining beach pea that nestled in the sandy folds of the windswept stone, and to listen to the hollow sound of the sea against the craggy shore.

~

"We can't really know anything till we get there," Cassie was saying. "We have no facts. We don't know how many guards will have been left in each town, or even how receptive the villagers will be."

The rebels were gathered in the center of the sleeping room. Although they'd eaten an early dinner, it was already getting dark.

"It will be dangerous work," Reba cautioned. "One misstep and all could be lost. But we're guessing the Rulers will try to get their armies back from the South before snowfall. That's our outside deadline."

"So mostly we'll work in pairs?" Maya asked.

"Yes. In pairs." It was a young woman from Bree's village who spoke now. "Except for in the villages where we already have support, where one person will be enough. Anyway, the first challenge will be to get inside the village walls."

"Like gophers," said Bree with a laugh. "Into the vegetable garden."

"You could say that. And it will help if the gophers are familiar with the villages they're going into."

"I'll take Village Seven," said Zena. "And I think I can do it alone. Lex has already laid a lot of the groundwork there."

"And," said Reba, "even though I haven't been there since I was young, I'll go to Village Three."

"Village Three will be a challenge. You'll need help there."

Reba nodded.

Village Three! It hadn't occurred to Leora that a return to Village Three would be part of the action. She didn't doubt for a minute that she'd be the one who would be accompanying Reba there. At first the thought filled her with alarm. But then, with growing excitement, she imagined entering the familiar gate in darkness; and the house, as they sneaked into it when all were asleep. She imagined waking Norie. How surprised she would be! To see not only her but, even more surprising, Reba! Norie could keep them hidden in Leora's old room by day, and by night . . .

Leora's thoughts were interrupted by a question from Bree to Reba. "So Leora will go with you to Village Three?"

"Well . . ."

In the pause, Leora felt a sinking in the pit of her stomach.

"The guards there are awfully familiar with Leora. I worry about putting . . ." Reba put her hand on her shoulder. "Leora, I haven't found you just to risk losing you again."

Leora avoided Reba's eyes.

"But we have a lot of support in Village Fifteen. And

you already know the del Valles. It's the safest place I can think of." Reba was talking quickly, whether to forestall the tears in her own eyes, or those in Leora's, Leora wasn't sure.

"Leora, I want you to be our gopher into Village Fifteen."

Good-bye

REBA, CASSIE, and Leora rowed off over a smooth morning sea, along with one other rebel who would row back for the next group. The groups, each on their way to a different village, would be spacing their arrivals to the mainland throughout the day, so as not to end up traveling together.

Leora had awakened that morning from a vivid dream. In the dream, she saw two land banks, separated by water. A massive army of red-coated guards gathered on the lower bank. Hoping the dream might hold information, she drew it, even embellishing the picture with a few dabs of wild strawberry juice to depict the guardsmen's uniforms.

When it was Cassie's turn to examine it, she said it showed the Rulers' army gathered on the far bank of the Nob River. Leora was disappointed. The rebels already knew that the guards had gone south, over the Nob River, on their way to the southern border. She had so wished to contribute some new information of special importance.

～

After the landing, the three of them retraced the route Leora had traveled in the spring. The rising sun outlined the occasional apple tree, heavy with fruit, and shone through the low scrub, here and there igniting a dull red blueberry bush into flaming scarlet. Like the color of fire, Leora thought.

As they picked their way through the low brush, Leora half hoped she might see Tomo ambling toward them out of the distance. Where was he? And where was Wiggala? And Howie? Reba thought it likely that the troops would have taken Howie along as a chopper on their mission to the southern border.

When they came upon Village Fifteen, the pointed tips of the stockade wall were lit by the sun. The silence seemed ominous. Leora felt a sudden chill, and wrapped her poncho around herself. She reminded herself that she would soon enjoy a warm welcome from Mrs. del Valle, who would probably be up before the rest of her family, preparing a hot breakfast.

"We have a special entrance through the wall," Reba was saying in a whisper now, leading the way to the west side of the village gates. "There's a missing bit of log in the fence. It opens into an abandoned shed at the dead end of an alleyway. From the front of the shed you'll be able to see the del Valles' house, in the opposite alley, down the road."

Reba had wrapped an arm around her. A lump came into Leora's throat. She dared not look at her sister.

"I'm sorry, Leora," Reba said. "It won't be long. You're more precious to me than anything, and I have to keep you as safe as I can. Whatever . . ."

Whatever happens, Leora knew she had been going to say.

Reba might never come back from Village Three.

As a rush of sobs got the best of Leora, her sister held her. At last Reba said, as if they were children again and trying to think of a good game to play, "I've got an idea!"

Leora forced her chest into stillness.

"Let's trade lockets!"

The idea was so silly and useless and pleasing that Leora giggled in her tears and nodded.

They each unclasped their chains. Reba reattached hers about Leora's neck and accepted Leora's in turn.

"Hurry up," Leora said, trying to be as matter-of-fact as a good rebel should be. "Or you'll be too late to get away."

"You go in first," Reba said. "Then we'll leave."

"Are we saying good-byes till the sun goes down?" barked Cassie, blinking quickly. "Don't do anything foolish, Leora."

"Bye, Cassie. Bye, Reba. Tell Norie I'm safe." And

with that she climbed into the darkness of the shed on the interior side of the stockade.

The air was still and musty. Her hand gave a quiver like an animal sensing danger. Ignoring it, she pushed open the creaking door of the tiny shed, and quickly spied the del Valles' egg-yolk yellow cottage.

The faint padding of her soft shoes on the dirt road seemed too loud.

Or was it that the town was too quiet?

Like a ghost town, she thought, hurrying her steps toward the yellow house.

No smell of breakfast welcomed her as she opened the door into their entryway. Her heart sank as she peered into an empty kitchen. On the table were signs of a meal half eaten. A pea soup, long since grown cold in the bowls, was crusted and dry.

She ran to Yano and Margarita's bedroom. The picture she had drawn of Margarita hung on the wall. It looked silently back at her. The bedroom beyond was also empty.

Making no effort now to muffle the slam of the door, she ran out of the house. She had to catch Reba and Cassie.

The houses stared at her with blank and silent eyes.

Nothing warned her of the presence of a figure that slid swiftly from behind the corner of a house and into her path. She slammed headlong into the shiny gold buttons of a red coat.

Caught

"JUST WHAT do you think you're doing here?"

Leora looked away quickly from a pudgy face, its carefully combed mustache all but obscuring a set of very long teeth. The guardsman was backed up by a second, a weasely little man with sleek black hair.

The rough hold on Leora's arms hurt, but, like an animal in danger, she froze. Her left hand was exposed but closed and clenched—not notable, she hoped.

"Your name," demanded the first, walrus-faced, guard.

Leora was silent.

"Your name, I said." The guard gave her a shake.

"Maybe he's mute," the second guard suggested.

Leora had forgotten that she must still look like a boy.

"Some of these creatures don't even speak English,"

her captor sneered. "What I'm wondering is how he escaped the roundup of men and boys. The troops needed all the help they could get."

"That one looks too weak and puny to carry munitions. They probably passed him by."

"So how did he escape being put with the women and girls and young ones in the hold, then? We've been through each house in the village three times over. He must have found himself a little hideaway we missed." The walrus shook her again. "Is that so?" Leora could feel his hot breath.

"Heading back to his hideaway, I'll bet he was," said the other one. "Just came out like a hungry rat to find himself some grub."

Leora's thoughts were on the shed through which she had entered the village. No more than five paces away, its door was half ajar. Her fear that Reba and Cassie might have left her behind was replaced by a hope that they were safely away.

"Aiming for that little shed there, I'll bet." The weasely guard headed for the doorway.

"What have we here? Our rat's got a hole in the wall."

Hoping to distract them, Leora threw herself into a fit of wild resistance. Fierce as a trapped raccoon was a phrase she'd heard Howie use more than once. She thrashed, snarled, and bared her teeth.

This only succeeded in producing a roar of surprise

from the walrus, and a tightening of his iron hold. A well-aimed kick, however, produced a yowl of pain, and sudden release. As her victim bent double, groaning and cursing, Leora sped out of the alleyway, away from the shed.

The weasel was upon her in ten strides. This time she found her arms twisted roughly behind her back, her wrists held together in a single viselike grip.

"Not so puny after all, eh?" the weasel said, slightly amused at his companion's expense.

As she was led back, the walrus resumed his full height and struck Leora an angry blow on the side of her head. "You little piece of dirt!"

Leora clenched her teeth. At least the shed had been forgotten.

"So how do you figure?" the small guard asked as he half pulled and half pushed Leora along the street. "If he got in from the outside, where did he come from? And how?"

"No, he's a village brat, all right. They all look alike," the larger guard said. "But still . . . there've been suspicions that these Fifteeners were plotting. I wouldn't put anything past them. We'll keep this one in the hold with the rest of them till the new Master of Intelligence gets back from the North. I think the rat could be convinced to say some very interesting things."

The hold, it turned out, was within the building just

between the grain silo and the village entry gates. Leora remembered seeing it before. She also remembered drawing it. But in her picture, the shape of the building had been obscured by flames.

Leora was shoved roughly within, then down a narrow set of stone stairs.

"We've an interesting little addition for your collection," said the weasel, clearly pleased with himself.

It was cold in the basement, and, except for a tiny hole of light near the ceiling, it was so dark that at first Leora could see nothing. As her eyes grew accustomed to the darkness, she made out the figures of three guardsmen lounging about a table, playing a game with matchsticks.

"Not much of a specimen. Where'd you find it?" asked the most disheveled of the crew, standing and pulling a great ring of keys from his pocket.

Leora had the impression of voices murmuring beyond a heavy door to the left. The sound ceased as the key ground in the lock. The door groaned on its hinges and yawned, revealing darkness.

"Well, laaaaadies," the doorkeeper said mockingly. "We have a . . . uh . . . gen-tle-man for your entertainment. Don't fight over him now." He snickered.

The guards guffawed as Leora found herself thrown headlong into an even darker, foul-smelling room.

As the door closed behind her with a squeal and a thud, two cloaked figures rose in the darkness and sprang toward her, lifting her gently, while murmuring in Spanish.

"Mrs. del Valle?" Leora said hopefully.

The two kindly faces that bent closely to her were strangers, she realized with a pang, but one turned, softly calling, "Mercedes," across the dark cellar.

"Leora!" an approaching figure exclaimed in astonishment.

Leora couldn't recognize her in the darkness, but Mrs. del Valle's voice was familiar and very welcome. Leora soon found herself being squeezed, comforted, and made much of as Mrs. del Valle moved her between the crouched and curious forms of women and children.

"My sister!" crowed a little figure who jumped up excitedly at Leora's approach.

"Shhh!" Mrs. del Valle warned.

"Margarita!" Leora cried as the child hurled herself toward her.

"And Yano?" Leora asked.

"They took him. They took them all. The men and the boys."

"Where?"

"To the border. To fight against Maynor's neighbors. They took them to carry the ammunition."

"When?"

"It's three days now. Then they collected all the women, girls, and little ones. They said people in our village are enemies of the Rulers. They were afraid we would make trouble while all the guards are away."

"When will they return?"

Mrs. del Valle shrugged, her body telling more than her words.

"What will happen when they come back?"

Again she shrugged, this time putting her finger to her lips and casting her eyes in Margarita's direction.

"And you?" Mrs. del Valle asked, quickly changing the subject. "What happened?"

Leora told her about being captured.

"And before that. Did you find what you were looking for?"

"Yes," said Leora. "I did."

"Ahhh. I am very glad."

"And," Leora said, "they . . . are working on . . . the situation."

"It has begun?" Mrs. del Valle said with surprise.

"Yes."

"But how can things be ready? I hope it is not too soon."

Leora, looking around at the roomful of women and children, and remembering her drawing of the fire, could only say, "I only hope it is not too late."

Prisoners

WHEN THE CHILDREN were asleep, Mrs. del Valle introduced Leora, in Spanish, to the women, who were wrapped in their shawls and crouching closely together for warmth. Leora wasn't exactly sure what Mrs. del Valle told them, but it was met with murmured exclamations, nods, and questions.

Leora told them all she knew. Excitement was followed by dismay as the women realized that it would be weeks before the rebels could possibly be returning in force. She saw in the despair in their faces that they had little hope of surviving till then.

How useless she felt, being a gopher into a prison. Far from being able to help with the revolution, she could not even help herself.

The break of day was heralded by only the tiniest increase in light through the barred window. As the morning wore on Leora noticed that from time to time, like the wind in the trees, a whispered wave of Spanish would sweep through the room, as each woman heard and relayed a message in turn.

"We take turns listening at the door," explained Mrs. del Valle. "For news. Mostly all we hear is bad jokes and ugly words," she continued. "But the troops send back runners from the front with news of progress. The last thing we learned was that the forces are to the south as far as the Nob River.

"Probably," she added sadly, "they are by now on the other side."

～

Time passed slowly in the dark room. The nights grew colder, and they were all hungry. The guards only visited once a day now, bringing a single meager meal: a sackful of crackers, and two jugs of water. An added frustration for the hungry prisoners was knowing that just over their heads, in the food-storage room, was the town's supply of winter food.

To distract them from their hunger, Leora spent the days entertaining Margarita and a bevy of other small children with tales and drawings of Wiggala.

"Weegala. More Weegala!" they cried, each time she thought she had already extracted every possible detail of her little friend from her memory.

When Leora had finally run out of paper and stories, Margarita and the other children concentrated on teaching Leora Spanish. Sometimes she deliberately flubbed her lessons to make them laugh.

But in reality there was no cause for humor.

Each day took the men of Village Fifteen farther south.

Each day brought the prisoners closer to the inevitable moment Leora feared—when the guards would light fire to the prison building.

And the rebels, by now dispersed to the various villages, would have barely begun secretly enlisting support.

Leora had no idea how many days had passed on the morning that the walrus-faced guard strode in, slammed down their miserable sack of crackers, and announced, "It's almost over. The new Master of Intelligence is expected back from the North any day now. He may have questions for you ladies."

"He'll definitely have questions for your little through-the-wall Romeo," chimed in the weasel, entering and depositing the water jugs with a slosh. "They say," he went on, scanning the darkness for Leora, "that the new Master is very good at questions."

"I've heard he's so eager he sometimes forgets to *ask* the questions before he . . . well . . ." The walrus lowered his voice, and added to his companion, "I wouldn't be in the boy's shoes for all that's holy."

"Well," said the weasel hastily, "I can tell you that

carrying water for the likes of these ones is not my idea of fun. I'll be glad when it's over."

"So," said Mrs. del Valle as the heavy door slammed behind the guards, "now we know why they keep us alive." Then she gasped. "Oh, Leora! Don't listen to me. I forget you are just a child."

But Mrs. del Valle's words only echoed Leora's own thoughts.

"The picture," she said simply, to let Mrs. del Valle know she understood the gravity of the situation.

"Back then we did not know the worst truth of that picture," Mrs. del Valle said. "That the people would be inside."

The fear in the room had grown thick. Children fretted. Babies cried. And mothers were quiet.

The smell had become almost unbearable. The women took turns standing by the single tiny window, catching a few minutes of fresh air, hoping beyond hope for a glimpse of a miracle.

Leora, climbing on a box in order to reach the barred opening, gazed out at the unchanging patch of shrubbery. She wished she could see through the bushes to the fields and the forest that she knew lay beyond.

She thought about the forest. She thought about Tomo, and Wiggala, and Mama Birmba. Where were they now? She longed for the feel of Wiggala's tiny hand.

A clearing in the sky brought a flush of light to the low cedar beyond the window, accentuating its twisting boughs. She found herself tracing the flowing lines in her mind, straining her eyes to decipher the complex texture of the flat needles as they rearranged themselves gently in the wind.

Her heart skipped a beat. Was it possible? Of course not!

For a fraction of a second she imagined that she had seen a pair of eyes in the tapestry of green. Strain and hunger must be getting to her, she thought.

"If wishes were fishes . . ." Howie would have said, "we'd have lobster for tea."

Howie. Undoubtedly he, along with the others, was now far beyond the Nob River.

Whether from exhaustion or despair, the women had given up their listening for news. So when there were sounds of commotion from the guards' room, several women rose hastily to their feet and moved to the door. Now all eyes were on the shawled figures who listened.

Before long, one of the listeners cried aloud. It was only with difficulty that she was able to articulate her bad news.

"She says," Mrs. del Valle translated for Leora, "that the bridge over the Nob River has fallen in pieces into the water."

"With everyone on the other side?"

Mrs. del Valle nodded.

"*Nunca*," the woman was wailing. "*Nunca, nunca.*"

Leora did not need a translator. They would never see their men and boys again.

For the rest of the long day, Yano's face hovered before her eyes.

～

As she drifted into sleep that night, a vague idea wound through the edges of her consciousness. Something about the bridge. What had it been? She tried to reconstruct the thought. But it escaped into the web of her dream.

Later that night Leora called out into the darkness.

Reba! Reba! Come back!

She awoke with the sound of her own voice in her ears. She thought she might have actually called out loud, but all around her the huddled villagers snored softly, and even Margarita, with her hand clasped loosely around Leora's finger, slept on.

The next days were the longest she had ever spent. Time seemed to stand still. The children, weak with hunger, huddled close to their mothers. The babies had stopped crying. The guards, perhaps sensing that the women had lost their will, no longer even troubled themselves to watch their charges at night.

Leora was now the lone sentinel at the little window. The cold autumn wind sang through the bushes. *Wishing for fishes, wishing for fishes*, it murmured ceaselessly. But wish as she might, she saw no eyes in the shrubbery.

Nor did the twisted boughs part to reveal any other form of salvation.

~

They seized her in the depths of her sleep. By the time she was fully awake she had been carried out of the dungeon's darkness into the torch-lit guards' room. The guards clearly intended to isolate her from her companions. And the women, exhausted by sorrow and fear, did not wake.

It was an unfamiliar guardsman who put her down, shut the door quietly, and turned the lock in the key. He pulled Leora closer to the pale light of a torch on the wall, holding her by the scruff of her neck like an animal.

"You don't really think this puny little specimen is a rebel, do you?"

"What's the difference?" said the walrus, yawning, clearly annoyed at having been roused from his bed. "They say the Master has a way of getting answers even from people who don't know them."

"Maybe questioning the child will improve the Master's spirits," the new guard mused. "He's not happy. He was attacked by birmbas. Just as he arrived, right outside the gate."

The walrus, suddenly fully awake, whistled. "For real?"

"Three of them. Though one was just a baby. But it was the baby that flew at him like a mad thing out of nowhere. You'd have thought the baby had something against him personally. He was lucky the beasts just whacked him about a bit."

"Mussed up his pretty jacket, did they?" said the walrus with a sneer.

"You'll watch that talk, if you know what side your bread is buttered on," the guard warned.

"He's not a Captain of Arms. Only a Master of Intelligence," the walrus scoffed.

"Well, I wouldn't cross him in the best of his moods," said the new arrival, lowering his voice at the sound of voices above. "And tonight he's mad as a hornet."

Leora had listened to the whole exchange without moving, almost without breathing. As footsteps descended the steps, she was overcome by the old wave of sickness. Even without seeing him, she knew exactly who the new Master of Intelligence was.

The guards jumped to their feet, saluted, and barked in unison.

"Master Blencher, SIR."

Master of Intelligence

"IS THERE no Captain in the village?" Wilfert demanded, trying to make out the guards on duty in the darkness.

"They all went south to the front, sir. We were left in charge."

Wilfert's eyes narrowed, calculating.

"Well, I'm in charge now, then, isn't that so?"

After only a moment's hesitation, the weasel swallowed and responded, "Yes, sir."

"Yes, *Captain*!" Wilfert corrected, pronouncing his new title with relish.

"Yes, Captain, sir."

Wilfert adjusted his coat and squared his shoulders.

"And why were there no guards outside the gate?" he demanded, his manner suddenly sterner, his voice a notch deeper.

"It has never been the practice, sir. Uhhhh, Captain, sir."

"Well, there were never birmbas right outside the gate either. Tomorrow I want every man in the barracks out hunting them. The beasts will pay! They'll be lucky if they die quickly!"

"And what have we here?" Wilfert said, seemingly soothed by his self-promotion, peering into the darkness where the guard still clutched Leora.

Leora was glad that the dim light of the single sputtering torch was at her back.

"Possibly a rebel, sir. Captain," said the walrus eagerly.

"A rebel!" Wilfert sneered. "If that's the rebels' best, we haven't much to fear."

"We found him days after the roundup, heading for a hole in the outer wall," wheedled the walrus. "If he knows about a hole in the wall, sir, we figure he knows some other interesting things, too. Captain, sir."

"Well, it wouldn't hurt to try," said Wilfert, cheered up, it seemed, by the prospect. "With so many of the forces on the other side of the Nob River, and the bridge down, the rebels might be tempted to try something very foolish.

"Yes," he continued. "I'll work on the boy myself. We need all the information we can get." Watching Leora through the dim light of the room, his hands began to twitch, as if they had already begun their task.

"My keys!" he exclaimed now, one roving hand discovering a broken clip on his belt. "They're missing!"

"Must have gotten lost out there in the attack," volunteered the newly arrived guard.

"Here," said Wilfert, roughly appropriating the weasel's jangling ring. "I'll take your set."

The weasel swallowed and blinked. "Yes, Captain."

Wilfert clicked the key ring to his belt. "Do we know if this creature speaks English?"

Leora could feel the walrus shrug. "Might, sir. Might not, sir. Don't know, sir. Captain."

"Filthy bit of rubbish, isn't it?" said Wilfert, squinting.

"Yes, sir. Captain."

"Well, I won't soil my hands with him tonight. It's good to be well rested for these things. And I'll be able to see him better by daylight. Throw him in a separate hold, the small one back there."

"And the women, sir?"

"There'll be nothing to learn from them. Women never know anything. We won't be needing them."

Leora was hit with a vivid image of the building in flames.

"Into the small cell with the boy," barked the weasel to the walrus, jerking his head toward a second door on the wall.

"I suppose you've been promoted, too," responded

the walrus under his breath, hauling Leora roughly to the second door off the guards' room.

Once again she found herself thrown headlong into a dark jail cell, the lock turning behind her. This time, however, she was quite alone.

Alone

LEORA CRAWLED to a side wall, crouching against it for its cold comfort. She made out the sound of retreating footsteps on the stairs. Wilfert had left. There wasn't the smallest doubt in her mind that, in the light of day, he would know her.

Before long, she heard the rest of the guards leave as well, and she was left in total silence.

This room, like the other, had a single small window, and as her eyes reaccustomed themselves to the darkness she could make out the dimensions of her new cell.

In size, it reminded her of the nook in the basement of the house in Village Three where Wiggala had been imprisoned. For a minute she was back in the cupboard watching Wilfert prodding the little ball of fur with his rod.

Her webbed hand, tucked in the crook of her leg, was clenched so tightly it ached.

A brightening of the moonlight revealed a stone bench beneath the window. Drawn to the opening, she climbed up and peered out into the night. From this window she could see past the wall of young cedar to the fields, the hill, and the forest beyond.

If wishes were fishes.

Well, maybe wishes *were* fishes. *She* knew which birmbas had attacked Wilfert.

A cloud drifted over the moon.

The night was just barely bright enough for her to make out a form moving down from the forest. It was a complicated shape, growing larger and smaller, until it evolved into several forms, which disappeared behind the low shrubs.

"Wishes *are* fishes!" she surprised herself by saying out loud.

And as promptly as if she had called Wiggala by name, a furry little form separated itself from the dark mass of the bush and loped to her window.

But did she hear something else out there?

"Quietly, quietly," she whispered joyfully, reaching her webbed hand out the window to stroke a very excited little birmba. "There's a guard out there somewhere. I heard his keys. Shush."

Wiggala seemed to understand her concern, and,

except for gently nuzzling her hand, stood quite still.

In a few moments, as the two stayed frozen there at the window, Leora found herself moving from delight to despair.

She had gotten her wish. But there was nothing the birmbas could do to help.

Tomorrow Wilfert would at last get his hands on her.

Tomorrow the guards would hunt down the birmbas.

Tomorrow all the prisoners could be burned alive.

Leora's hand squeezed Wiggala's little snout and tickled a silky ear. Wiggala, in response, hurled himself at the bars of the window.

The clatter of metal against metal startled Leora.

It was Wiggala that had jangled!

"*Shhh!*" she whispered urgently, her hand feeling for and finding the noisy item: a hefty ring of shiny keys on a chain around Wiggala's neck.

"Wiggala! You silly thief. Whose keys have you stolen?"

Even as the words left her mouth, she knew.

"Wiggala! You have Wilfert's keys!" The keys would almost certainly unlock the cells in which both she and the rest of the villagers were imprisoned, but rattling around Wiggala's neck, they would also make the baby birmba an easy, noisy target for the guards to track and kill.

Wiggala was busily tugging her hair, apparently hoping to pull her out through the bars.

"You have to give me the keys, Wiggala," Leora coaxed, stroking him with her left hand and gently maneuvering the chain with her right.

Wiggala was suddenly reluctant. He leaped back, clutching his shiny treasure with both paws.

"Oh no! Wiggala! Please!"

Wiggala paused.

Her next move was critical.

Crooning steadily to him, she searched the all-but-empty sack at her waist. Her fingers found the cool smoothness of Margarita's barrette.

Slowly, cautiously, she extended her offering to the window. She moved it this way and that, hoping the shiny bit of metal would glint in the moonlight.

Wiggala stood transfixed. Leora tapped the hair clip temptingly against the bars. Wiggala released the necklace of keys with one paw, still clutching it with the other, and approached warily.

"I'm not just going to give it to you, Wiggala," Leora said. "It's a trade."

Wiggala looked from Leora's face to the hair clip and stretched out a paw to receive it. Leora put her webbed hand on his shoulder and stroked his soft fur, remembering how they had laughed and hiccuped together in the grass.

"I need the keys more than anything, Wiggala," Leora said. "And the guards will find you and hurt you if you go clattering around with them."

Wiggala seemed to understand the deadlock.

"Please, Wiggala," she pleaded.

She heard a tiny sigh, the keys rattling as the baby birmba's grip loosened. Then she lifted the chain as Wiggala's eager fingers curled around the coveted clip. He sniffed it, licked it, and held it for a minute in his mouth. Taking it back out, he examined it in the moonlight and rubbed it happily against his cheek.

Then his snout was back between the bars, his tiny fingers trying again to pull Leora out through the window by her hair.

"Wiggala," said Leora, wanting nothing more at that moment than to take her little friend into her arms, "you and Tomo and your mama have to get away from here. They'll be looking for you tomorrow. With guns. Bang, bang. Go back to the woods. I'll find you later. I promise. Please go, Wiggala."

She put her webbed hand on his head, praying he would understand. After another little sigh, with many stops and many looks backward, the little birmba made for the dark folds of the shrubbery. Then, with two large shadows for company, his small form slid from bush to bush up the hill to the forest.

"Good-bye," she whispered, the keys cold and heavy in her hand.

She rubbed her locket thoughtfully. For the first time since she'd been in prison, she remembered it wasn't her own. It was Reba's. The locket with the sword.

She wished Reba were here.

But Reba wasn't.

Someone else would have to take charge.

Leora's Plan

AT FIRST, when Leora roused the women in the darkness, they were like a nest of hibernating animals, disoriented, disbelieving. Now, huddled around her, they were thoroughly awake.

"So let me understand, Leora," one of them said. "You say we will take the food from the storage room." In the darkness, Leora could barely make out the woman's hand pointing upward at the ceiling of the jail room. "And we will put it into the ammunition building down the street."

"Yes," said Leora.

"And then," a second woman chimed in, "we will take all that ammunition and bring it back here and put it where the food was."

"Exactly," Leora answered. "That way, when the guards light fire to this prison building, as they plan to do, they will destroy their own ammunition. But the food will be safe in the other building."

"What makes you believe that they will light fire to this building?" one woman asked.

"There is no time to explain that," Mrs. del Valle interrupted urgently. "We must do it all before dawn. But as Leora says, a few of you must take the children up the hill into the forest immediately. We will find you there when we're done."

Grateful that the guards no longer took the trouble to watch them at night, Leora carefully locked the door of the larger cell behind them. The door of her own, smaller, cell she left ajar.

Out in the open, Leora, along with the rest, paused to breathe in the fresh night air, and to marvel at the great expanse of starry sky overhead.

When they'd seen the children safely out the village gates, Leora and the others crept through the silent streets toward the ammunition building. The windowless storehouse was, they knew, right next door to the guards' sleeping barracks. As they drew nearer, they agreed to take turns standing in front of the barracks to listen for signs of life within. If any of the guards awoke, at least they'd have warning.

For two hours, they scurried past one another in the darkness, moving as silently and steadily as an army of ants. The powder and shells were gradually replaced with food, while in the room above the prison the pile of food dwindled as the mound of ammunition grew.

The loads were heavy, and Leora was afraid that exhaustion and starvation would make it impossible. But it seemed that some combination of fear and excitement kept everyone going.

When at last the job was done, the smell of sweat, gunpowder, and hastily munched apples mingled in the darkness of the food storage room.

"If this works, Leora," said Mrs. del Valle, contemplating the mound of munitions in the darkness, "for one little gopher, you will have done quite a lot of damage."

~

By sunrise they were all gathered up the hill in the shadows of the forest's edge. Leora spotted Wilfert as he headed out of the barracks and toward the prison. Even though she knew that she was safely concealed, her heart pounded in alarm at the sight of him.

"We should follow the others into the woods," she whispered.

"Yes," said Mrs. del Valle.

But along with half a dozen of the other women, she stood transfixed behind the screen of cedar boughs, unable to resist watching what they all hoped would be the successful unfolding of the plan.

Within seconds of Wilfert's disappearance into the prison building, the wind brought them the first howl of fury.

"It has begun," said Mrs. del Valle.

Wilfert's figure shot back out through the door.

"He was only in there for a moment," said Leora. "In that time he could have only learned that my cell is empty. He must still think the rest of you are in the one we left locked."

At first Wilfert seemed unsure what to do, flailing about like a marionette with tangled strings. But evidently his desire to blame someone prevailed, and as he disappeared in the direction of the barracks, the freed prisoners heard his rapid-fire abuses.

Within minutes, a dozen guardsmen, sleepily donning their coats, poured into the streets of Village Fifteen.

It was Wilfert himself, brandishing a burning torch, who set fire to the turreted prison building.

Up on the hill, no one spoke. Leora wondered how long it would take till the pile of munitions, now upstairs, would ignite.

"Look," said Mrs. del Valle, pointing off beyond the western edge of the village. "Do you see something?"

Leora strained her eyes. Yes. There was something moving in the shadow outside the village wall. There were men there. More than just a few. Could it be a contingent of guardsmen, returning unexpectedly from their mission to the South? Her heart sank. Could all the troops be returning? The rebels had been counting on the absence of most of the Rulers' troops to gain control of the villages. This could spell disaster to that carefully laid plan.

But something didn't make sense. "They're not wearing red coats," Leora observed.

Whatever the group was, its approach was obscured by the smoke from the growing blaze.

"It could only be guards," said Mrs. del Valle sadly. "And we better be getting away from here," she added, though she made no move to do so.

Under the cedar trees, they felt the wind shift.

"Santa Maria!" Mrs. del Valle gasped as the smoke changed direction to reveal the new arrivals as a straggling line of men and boys, each armed with a stick or a cudgel, moving stealthily toward the northeastern corner of the village's outer wall.

"Santa Maria!" Mrs. del Valle exclaimed again, clutching Leora's shoulder and shaking it harder and harder in her excitement. "It is our husbands! It is our sons! There are no troops with them. They must have escaped. They have come back to save us!"

Leora had a sudden frightening thought. "Did the men know that you were all imprisoned in the cellar of the food storage building?" she asked urgently.

"They knew!" gasped Mrs. del Valle. "They'll think we're still in there. They'll try to save us! They'll burn instead of us!"

As the women watched, the first man in the straggling line of returning villagers rounded the corner of the wall. For a moment the ragged pack stood still. Then the word appeared to fly through their ranks, and, as one, the men and boys of Village Fifteen tore desperately toward the burning building.

Propelled by this sight, the women on the hilltop burst out of their hiding place and, with frantic cries, went pounding down the hill. Toward the village, toward their husbands and sons . . . and toward a troop of the Rulers' armed guards.

Battle

WITH THE ARRIVAL of the village men, Leora heard Wilfert barking orders, bringing guardsmen into the streets like a swarm of angry wasps.

But when he spotted the women running down the hill toward him, Leora saw him freeze. Then he dashed through the rising smoke, peering down through the dungeon windows into the empty prison room below.

"Fetch arms! Fetch arms!" he shouted, sending the unarmed red-coated guards scurrying back to the sleeping barracks for their guns.

Leora, foremost of the runners, made out Yano and his father turning in through the village gate.

"Yano!" she shouted. "We're safe!"

At the sound of a young voice speaking English, Wilfert spun around.

"You!" he cried, sighting his recently escaped victim.

Then, in the full light of day, he finally recognized her.

"YOU!" he thundered. "MUTANT!"

Wilfert charged toward Leora, apparently ready to strangle her with his bare hands. He might have reached her, but Yano's hastily outstretched foot brought him gracelessly to the dirt.

In the time it took Wilfert to regain his footing, Yano had dragged Leora and his mother behind a building. Around them, Leora could see women busily informing their men of the facts: The dungeon was empty; and the food storage room upstairs from it was full. Full of explosive munitions.

"We thought the bridge over the Nob River was down," Mrs. del Valle cried, tears streaming down her face at the sight of her son. "How did you get back here?"

"One night, when we were on the far side of the river, we took their bags of gunpowder. We ran back over to this side, all of us together. Then we used their powder to explode the bridge!"

"So it is the *army* that cannot get back to this side!" said Mrs. del Valle, shouting above the growing sound of musket fire. She looked at her son as if she were seeing him for the first time.

"*Sí, Mamá.* But you two should get back up that hill where it is safe. I must go and fight."

Then he was gone.

Peering around the corner of a building, Leora and Mrs. del Valle could see that the guards had reappeared and were wasting no time in using their weapons. The air was torn by the roar of musket fire. The villagers— men and boys, now joined by some of the women— were racing to take cover from the danger of the burning building.

It was Mr. del Valle who now appeared out of the smoke. With a look of gratitude and relief, he hugged his wife.

"Leora," he said breathlessly. "Your friend Howie is with us. He's coming in through a hole in the wall in the south end of the village. With more men."

"We'll need every one of them," said Leora, glad to hear that Howie was near, but dismayed to see how many red coats had poured into the streets. A huge number of them must have arrived from the north with Wilfert the night before. Even if they ran out of ammunition, the guards would still outnumber the villagers.

The fire at the storage building had been slow to spread. Only now did its timbers begin to crackle loudly. Would it explode?

"Our first job," said Mr. del Valle, distancing them still further from the danger of the burning building, "will be to tease them till their ammunition is gone.

"But you, *Mamacita*," he said urgently. "Someone will have to take care of Margarita, if . . . I want you away from the fighting." As shots splintered the wall behind them, Mr. del Valle pressed them around the corner.

"And, Leora," he added. "I'm sure you're a good fighter. But whether we win or lose this one, you have a special gift. We need you for the future of Maynor. So go now, please, both of you! Up the hill!"

With that, Mr. del Valle ran back into the smoke.

Leora was ready to give up being in charge, for now. But she could not bring herself to leave.

"You go on!" she cried to Mrs. del Valle. "Find the children. I'll meet you in the forest soon."

Mrs. del Valle leaned close to Leora to make herself heard. "There will be many hurt. I will find sheets from the houses for bandages and help with the wounded. We will set up a place just up there," she pointed, "within the woods."

Looking around, Leora could see from the number of bleeding and disabled villagers that there was already a need for such help.

"I'll just wait for Howie's group to arrive," Leora called over the din. "Then I'll be up to help, with more cloth for bandages."

Leora ducked into a nearby house. Its walls lent protection from the furor outside, and for a moment, in its silence, she could sense the presence of its missing inhabitants. It reminded her of how she'd felt in the del Valles' house. She only hoped, when all was done, that they would all once again occupy their homes. Then, seizing a rough woven sack, she got to work.

Moving from one building to the next as she collected cloth, Leora saw the rebels teasing out the guards' ammunition. The deafening bursts of musket fire combined with the accelerating crackle of the burning storage building. She strained her eyes for a glimpse of Yano or Mr. del Valle, but couldn't see them. Her nostrils were filled with the smell of gunpowder and her lungs with the sting of smoke.

A great hullabaloo at the opposite end of town signaled the arrival of what Leora supposed must be Howie's group. Just in time. She thought she saw Howie through the smoke, even as she heard Wilfert's voice, calling for more ammunition.

For the first time that morning, guards thronged to the munitions building. Leora tried to imagine their surprise as they confronted a room full of potatoes! It must have been just as they did that the munitions, back in the burning building, ignited at last.

It started with a few random explosions and a great display of sparks. Then, with a sound of thunder that made the earth tremble, the entire building blew sky-high.

The guards, stunned, simply stopped and stared.

A spontaneous cheer rose from the villagers.

"LEORA!" She heard the voices of some of the women shouting her name.

"LEO-RA! LEO-RA!" More villagers echoed the cry.

After that, the villagers wasted no time in pressing

their advantage, hefting their cudgels and sticks with enthusiasm. The guardsmen, deprived of ammunition, milled in confusion, unsure how to fend for themselves without the protection of their guns.

Keeping to the fringe of the violence, Leora spread the word about getting the wounded out of the battle area, helping everyone she found who had been hurt to make their way safely up the hill. When she had a chance, she delivered more bandages and brought bucket after bucket of water to the makeshift hospital in the woods.

"Stay, Leora," said Mrs. del Valle, deftly tourniqueting the bleeding hand of one of the two dozen wounded villagers sheltered in the shadow of the cedars. "We cannot risk losing you."

"I'll just go one more time," said Leora. "I haven't found Howie yet."

Down below, she saw that the guards' frustration had translated into fury. Using their muskets as clubs, they were now attacking viciously.

As Leora emerged from a house with a new supply of bandages, she nearly stumbled over a fallen villager in front of the door. Barely conscious, he was not much bigger than Yano. Using all her strength, she was able to drag him into the relative safety of the house. She could do no more for him.

Reemerging, she looked around her with growing concern. The number of bleeding and wounded seemed to have grown far beyond what she could help with. The villagers had spent what little advantage they had. Defeat, she saw, was just a matter of time.

Suddenly a familiar voice shouted her name.

It was Howie, running toward her, his face blackened by smoke and ash, his hand bleeding.

"Leora! You have to go! There is no time left!"

"Oh, Howie!" she cried. "They can't beat us! They mustn't!"

Then, remembering her good news, she said, "I found her, Howie! I found Reba! She's got the rebels training and recruiting in the villages. The revolution has begun."

Howie stopped and gave her a grin. Leora grinned back.

"What a splendor you are! And it *has* begun!"

His face grew grim as he looked around. "It's too late for us here today, I'm afraid. But who knows? It may not be too late for Maynor."

Leora, too, looked around.

"They just can't beat us, Howie!"

"You've done a grand job so far, Leora!" Howie said, his own eyes clouding. "Your father would have been proud of you! Proud of the two of you.

"But go now," he pleaded. "Someone will have to lead the women and children back to that old Town Hall in the forest. It's the only safe shelter, and you know the way. We'll buy you all the time we can."

Leora's eyes lit on a scene ten yards away. Mr. del Valle, his back to the wall, his head bloody, was trying to fend off the blows of two guards.

"No!" Leora cried, lunging toward him.

Howie's arm barred the way.

"Go!" he cried. "We need you to safeguard the others!"

Leora could barely nod. She knew he was right, but it took all the willpower she possessed to turn her back and leave.

"Leora!" he called after her.

Tears coursed through the soot on his face.

"Tell Norie . . . she was my turtledove."

Leora could only nod. Then from alleyway to alleyway, struggling against the pull of all that held her there, she forced her legs to carry her toward the village gate.

Arrival

BLINDED BY smoke and tears as she emerged from the village, Leora didn't see them at first. It was the murmur, like the sound of a rushing river, that drew her eyes to the hill above. They came out from the forest in a trickle, but in seconds their numbers had swelled into a torrent.

They were white and brown and black. They were men and women. Each brandished a crude weapon: a club, a staff, a knife, or a hatchet.

Not dozens. Hundreds. Hundreds and hundreds. It wasn't just rebels, Leora thought. It was *the people*!

At first Leora did not see Reba in their midst.

But suddenly, there she was, her wild curly hair blowing in the wind. With tears streaming down her face, she swept Leora into her arms.

"We were afraid we were too late," Reba shouted over the din.

"How did you know to come?"

"We had gathered at Town Hall. You know the place. Then we heard an explosion and saw the smoke. We got here as fast as we could. What exploded?"

"Their ammunition. We hid it in the building they planned to set on fire," Leora shouted.

"We couldn't have done better! They have no munitions!" Reba cried, turning to those around her. "We must keep them from getting across the river and warning the troops to the south!"

"It won't be a problem. The bridge at the Nob River is down!" said Leora.

"So it really *is* down!" Reba said in astonishment, rubbing Leora's locket, which she still wore about her neck. Then, searching the crowd, she called, "Bree! Maya!"

The two pushed their way to the forefront, hugging Leora and firing questions all at once.

Leora, suspecting that her sister was about to ask them to protect her, grinned. "Don't worry. I'm fine. I need to get these bandages to Mrs. del Valle. She's taking care of the wounded up the hill. Go."

Reba looked hard at her, then nodded.

Leora watched as the three of them, clearly eager for battle, stormed into the thick of things. It wasn't long before she saw Bree in the distance, skillfully wielding her staff as she cornered the walrus, who, using his musket clumsily as a club, tried in vain to defend himself.

Not far off, Cassie was busy inflicting serious damage on not one, but two, extremely surprised guardsmen.

It was a very different Howie who now accosted her joyfully.

"This is more like it!" he cried. "What a mutiny, Leora! What a grand smashing mutiny!" And with that he charged back into the fray.

By now, Leora could see, the guards were in a state of total disarray. Wilfert, who should have been in command, was nowhere in sight.

It would not have surprised Leora if he had deserted his own men—run away to save his own skin once he saw that the tide of battle had turned.

Hefting her sack of cloth, she mounted the hill toward the shelter of the woods. Exhaustion was getting the best of her, and the smoke was making her sick.

Entering the darkness of the woods, she felt a familiar chill.

It was a feeling she knew all too well.

She saw the flash of red and the brass buttons before she made out his features. His arm was around her neck before she had a chance to scream.

"So it's you and me now," Wilfert whispered, his breath hot in her ear.

Even if a scream could have been heard above the din, her voice was stopped by the tightening of his arm. Clearly fearful of once again losing his prey, he maneuvered her deeper into the woods, away from the sound of women's voices.

Throwing her against a tree, Wilfert held her by the throat with one hand and, with the other, made a grab for her left arm.

His face, masklike, was blackened by soot. His grimace of a smile revealed his tiny pointed teeth. Her webbed hand, as he touched it, sensed the full extent of his cruelty.

"So tell me, LEO-RA. Why did the people shout your name when the building exploded?" His fingers were busy trying to pry open the fingers of her clenched webbed hand, which now trembled uncontrollably.

Leora could feel herself shrinking, dissolving, as she had so often in Wilfert's presence. She remembered sights from long ago: of the bird, brought down by Wilfert's slingshot, lying stunned and helpless on the ground; and of the little pile of feathers on the basement floor.

The sounds of battle seemed a million miles away now. Strength was draining out of her like stuffing from a doll. Overwhelmed with sickness, her knees buckling, Leora felt herself sinking into darkness.

At first the darkness was overwhelming, an empty and lonely space.

But mysteriously, it began to change.

Now it was like the night sky; like the ocean from

which she had pulled Reba. It was some vast place from which everything came and everything went.

Another image came to her now.

She could see, as she had back at the island, a picture of the people gathered together in Town Hall. She heard their voices, joined together into a single sound like the roar of the wind in the maple.

Leora felt the immense invisible world that lay beyond her hand, and for the first time, she was not frightened. She felt its power lifting her and filling her limbs with strength. "It doesn't matter what you do to me," she said. "The people will win."

"The people!" Wilfert spat. "They are sheep. We will defeat them, crush them. They have no power."

"You think cruelty is power," said Leora. "It is only cruelty."

She thought of the name León, as the del Valles pronounced it. Lion.

"You cannot do anything to me," she said, wresting her hand with a powerful twist from Wilfert's prying fingers.

"I can do everything to you. You are nothing." Wilfert made a grab again for her hand. "You are worse than nothing. You are a *defective*!"

And then an unexpected thing happened. In Leora's mind, Wilfert suddenly appeared to her as the young, ignorant, bragging boy he had been when he shot the bird with his slingshot.

"Defective?" she said. The strong feeling inside her now was as still and smooth as the morning sea.

"Defective?" she said again, looking through him, past his brass buttons and beyond his mean little eyes into a place that was empty of everything but fear, hatred, and ignorance.

"You don't know what defective means," she said.

Wilfert froze, taken aback by her words. Or something he saw in her eyes.

The silence was broken by a terrible snarl and a crash from the woods nearby. Wilfert let go of Leora just in time to see Tomo charging toward them, teeth gnashing and paws raised.

"Not me!" Wilfert cringed as he stumbled backward. "Not *me*! Get *her*!"

Then Tomo gave Wilfert a swat that sent him sprawling onto the forest floor. Wilfert scrambled to his feet, and, howling with fear, fled into the woods with Tomo in furious pursuit.

Soon enough, Leora knew, she would get her chance to thank her friend. Meanwhile, listening to the sound of Wilfert's retreat, Leora couldn't help thinking of Tomo's father: surely shot by the guards. Like her own.

She massaged her webbed fingers. And looking down to the village below, where Reba stood tall among the fighting throngs, she thought that Howie was right.

Her father would have been proud of his daughters.

Tales to Tell

THERE WERE many tales to tell when it was all over. Most of them were told in the warmth of Mrs. del Valle's kitchen, which was filled all day with the sweet smell of cornmeal cooking in its own husks.

Sooner or later that day, everyone was in that kitchen. Except, Leora kept remembering, the birmbas. She would find them, she knew, in the woods before long.

Lex—or Soaring Bird, as Leora liked to think of him—began by presenting Leora with a quill, a dusky blue-gray feather with a finely shaped brass tip, especially made for her by a woman in his village. It did not take Leora long to put it to good use, with Yano and Bree peering over her shoulder.

Then Yano, Howie, and Mr. del Valle, his head well

bandaged, told the story of the destruction of the bridge over the Nob River.

"We would never have dared to desert the troops if we still thought the birmbas were dangerous," Yano concluded. "But Howie told us about your friendly birmbas. So we prayed that he hadn't just dreamed it all, and we took the gunpowder and left."

There was a sadness in Cassie's face that Leora understood; for the Institute, with Cassie's brother in it, was on the other side of the Nob River—territory still securely in the hands of the Rulers.

Reba's tale, from so many years back, was told again from the very beginning. Leora joined in to tell the others all that had happened from the time she first saw the eyes in the orchard.

As she spoke, her eagerness to find the birmbas grew. She had already promised an eager Margarita that she would get a personal introduction to Wiggala before the week was out. And Margarita, proud that it was her own hair clip that had saved the day, was already collecting more shiny things to give to the little birmba when they met.

"But we still haven't heard why you rebels came back so soon," said Mrs. del Valle. "With so many people. In time to save us."

It was Cassie who began this tale.

"I'll leave you to imagine Reba's reunion with

Norie," she started off, her eyes warming at the memory. "And how Norie greeted the news of Leora's safety. But then, since we couldn't be sure Reba wouldn't be recognized, we decided to keep her presence a secret."

"Norie kept me hidden in your room," Reba whispered as an aside to Leora.

"As for me," Cassie continued, "I arrived at the governor's own doorstep—your old doorstep, Leora, that is—pretending to be the Head Ruler's very own niece. I had a finely penned letter—if I can brag a little—from the Head Ruler himself: recalling the governor to the capital to be named as *the new Vice-Ruler of Northeast Maynor.*"

Howie could not repress a guffaw. "And he *believed* it?"

"Oh, *how* he believed it!" said Cassie. "And his wife. And Tanette. How *they* believed it!

"The fuss those two made! Lording it over everyone. They couldn't resist a grand evening gala, assembling the governors and the muckety-mucks from five of the six local villages, with guard escort supplied. Just to rub it in.

"All went well with the gala until it was almost over, when an angry note from the governor of Village Six arrived, saying they were fools—the Head Ruler *had* no niece!"

Howie crowed. "Sucked the air right out of their sails, I'll bet."

"You can picture it. I've never seen three people so deflated. Luckily Norie had overheard the delivery of the message, so you can imagine I went undercover very quickly.

"But they were so humiliated, they vanished bag and baggage that night. With just a few guards and a chopper."

"But still," said Mrs. del Valle, "how did you know to come back so soon? We thought you would be weeks or months."

Now the tale fell to Reba.

"Well, for one thing, gathering support was easier than we could ever have dared to hope. The governor's departure from Village Three helped a lot. And what's more, there was a certain Miss Young—who by the way was very glad to hear you were well, Leora—who had already begun a little rebellious activity on her own.

"But as to what made us hurry so . . . well. That last drawing you did, Leora—of the two banks of a river, with the troops on the other side? I hadn't known what it was about. But one night I went to sleep holding your locket. And in my dream, I heard you calling me, telling me it was time to come back. When I woke up the next morning, I realized: in your drawing, there was no *bridge* between the banks. Most of the guards in Maynor were on the other side of the river, and no matter what we did on this side of the river, *they couldn't get back!*"

"I thought she had lost her mind," said Cassie. "She sent messengers to the rebels in all the villages telling them to meet at the old Town Hall in the forest with whatever people they had already been able to muster."

"I knew it was urgent," said Reba. "I told them," she said with embarrassment, "that it was safe to go, unprepared as we were, because the bridge *had* fallen. I was that sure of it," she said, rubbing Leora's locket, which she still wore about her neck.

"We almost divided over that one," said Cassie. Then she added sadly, "Especially since, I guess, I didn't *want* to believe that bridge was down with the Institute on the other side."

The room fell silent with this reminder that, beyond the bridge, there was work yet to be done.

"Show them your new drawing, Leora," whispered Yano.

All eyes were upon her.

She turned over an ivory page from the table before her and smoothed it out on the center of the table.

Everyone stood to get a better view.

In rich black ink, the flowing lines showed a boat, with three people in it and a sailful of wind, traveling between two shores.

"It's the shores of the Nob River," Reba said, recognizing the topography from the earlier drawing.

"And the bonniest boat I'll ever see," said Howie, looking lovingly at the lines of the vessel.

"This is you, Howie," Leora said, pointing at one of the three figures. "And this is you, Cassie, with your staff in the air. And this is me." In the picture, her own hand was pointed into the wind, its web clearly defined.

On the northern shore, enlarged out of all proportion, was a building that she recognized as Town Hall. Here, a figure she knew to be Reba's addressed a peaceful crowd.

On the southern shore stood a larger, grim structure of stone, a cloud of darkness enveloping it. "The Institute," whispered Cassie.

Standing out from the other figures in the dark structure were the forms of two boys.

"This one," said Leora. "His name is Jem."

"That's my brother's name!" said Cassie.

"At least we know he's alive and well," interjected Reba.

"And this one," Leora went on, "why . . . he *has* no name!"

"Well, Leora," said Reba, "I'm sure you'll find it out if anyone can."

"When we liberate the Institute?" said Cassie, a new note of hope in her voice.

"Yes," said Leora. "When we liberate the Institute."

Last

IT WAS NEARLY sundown when Leora, bearing a large knapsack on her back, climbed the hill to the forest's edge in hopes of finding the birmbas.

She had left Reba, along with islanders and villagers, making plans for a meeting at Town Hall. They all knew that there were difficult decisions and uncertain times ahead.

But for now, Leora allowed herself the pleasure of the sweet smell of cedar, and scanned the woods eagerly for a sight of her friends.

Wiggala must have been waiting for her. He came barreling out of the darkness like a small cannonball and threw himself into her arms with an exuberant squeal.

"You did it, Wiggala! You saved us all!"

Leora squeezed the furry bundle of excitement. She

stroked a silky ear with her webbed hand. Wiggala, with a small sprint, was over her shoulder and astride her knapsack, as if ready to travel. With his tiny fingers now caressing her own ears, she ventured farther into the woods, in the direction of the unexpected but unmistakable sound of Howie's voice.

"What a grand smashing mutiny it was, mate!" Howie was saying . . . to . . . to Tomo! "You should have seen it!" Howie was gesticulating. "We had them routed, heading for the lifeboats, the scurvy tars!"

Howie, seeing Leora, leaped to his feet, coughing and blushing at being found telling a story to a birmba.

But Leora had no qualms about talking to a birmba.

"Tomo!" she cried. "I've missed you!" And as soon as her webbed hand stroked his great furry arm, she knew that Tomo understood without words what was important. He looked at her with soft widened eyes, before being overcome by the biggest attack of itchy fleabites ever.

"Reba brought us something from Norie," Leora said, opening her knapsack, despite Wiggala's help.

"That's my Nor!" said Howie, hoisting the bag of somewhat squashed blueberry tarts and offering it around. "Mates?"

The bag was nearly empty, and Wiggala was stroking Leora's cheek with sticky purple fingers, when their feast was interrupted by a burst of song.

It was a pure sweet-throated call, the flutelike voice

lilting upward, then dwindling to a distant haunting tremolo. Just when Leora feared the song was done, the voice echoed itself, sliding its harmony into a new key.

It was like a waterfall going backward.

"Belay me," said Howie. "It's the hermit thrush!"

"It's singing!" Leora cried.

Howie eyed Leora happily.

"That she is," he said.